"I don't want you here. Go away and leave me alone."

She was in so much pain she was contradicting herself. He could resist a lot, but Hannah's pain brought down the final wall. He had to do something—at least try.

What could he say to make it better? Could he help her? Scott placed a hand on her shoulder, feeling the inflexible muscles. As if she were a troubled child he began moving his hand in comforting circles along her back.

"Hannah, I'm not leaving."

She stilled.

"Look, you're a fighter. And if Jake is anything like you, he is too."

He wrapped an arm around her shoulders and pulled her to him. She stiffened and pushed against his chest. "Let me help you get through this." His grip tightened and he tucked her head under his chin. Holding her as close as the chairs would allow, he said in a tender voice, "Let me be your friend. You need someone…"

Dear Reader

I fell in love with Scott and Hannah long before they fell in love with each other. Their story has been with me for years, and I'm proud to share it with you. Scott and Hannah are two intelligent, well-educated and independent people, who think they need no one but soon learn that love is a bond they can't break.

Writing Scott and Hannah's story has been an emotional journey for me. In many ways their story was an easy one to tell, while in others a difficult one. I know personally what it's like to have a child waiting for a new heart. My youngest son received the life-giving gift of a heart transplant when he was one year old. He is now twenty-two and doing well.

I would be remiss in following my convictions if I didn't take this opportunity to encourage you to think about organ donation. Transplants do save lives.

I hope you enjoy reading about Scott and Hannah. I'd be honoured to hear from you. You can find me at www.susancarlisle.us

Warmest regards

Susan

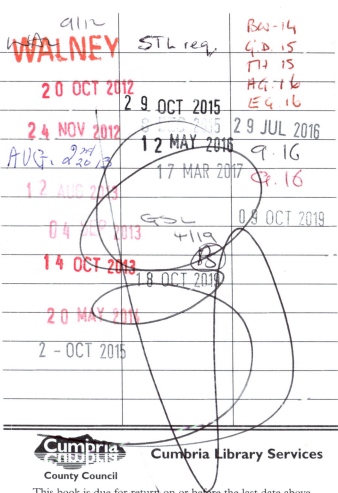

HEART SURGEON, HERO...HUSBAND?

BY
SUSAN CARLISLE

First published in Great Britain 2012
by Mills & Boon, an imprint of Harlequin (UK) Limited.
Large Print edition 2012
Harlequin (UK) Limited, Eton House,
18-24 Paradise Road, Richmond, Surrey TW9 1SR

© Susan Carlisle 2012

ISBN: 978 0 263 2245 97

Harlequin (UK) policy is to use papers that are natural, renewable and recyclable products and made from wood grown in sustainable forests. The logging and manufacturing process conform to the legal environmental regulations of the country of origin.

Printed and bound in Great Britain
by CPI Antony Rowe, Chippenham, Wiltshire

Susan Carlisle's love affair with books began when she made a bad grade in maths in the sixth grade. Not allowed to watch TV until she brought the grade up, she filled her time with books and became a voracious romance reader. She has 'keepers' on the shelf to prove it. Because she loved the genre so much, she decided to try her hand at creating her own romantic worlds. She still loves a good happily-ever-after story.

When not writing, Susan doubles as a high school substitute teacher—she has been doing this for sixteen years. Susan lives in Georgia, with her husband of twenty-eight years, and has four grown children. She loves castles, travelling, cross-stitching, hats, James Bond and hearing from her readers.

This is Susan's debut title for Mills & Boon® Medical™ Romance

'A heart-wrenching story of love and loyalty. Thank you, Ms. Carlisle, for sharing your story with us through Scott and Hannah and showing us the many ways that true love can win.'

—Goodreads on
Heart Surgeon, Hero...Husband? 5 stars

In Raina's Memory

* * *

Special Thanks

To my Tuesday night critique group for
steering me in the right direction each week,
especially Lisa and Claudia.

To my editor, Flo Nicoll, for
seeing something in my writing that
showed promise and encouraging me until that
something showed through. I appreciate you.

To Darcy for saying you should write this.
You were right.

To Sia for sharing your writing knowledge.
I'm better for it.

To Carol for reading, re-reading, and taking
care of me. Couldn't have done it without you.

To my mom, my husband and my kids
for being so supportive. I love you all.

CHAPTER ONE

"A HEART TRANSPLANT? My baby's only two years old." Hannah Quinn stared at Dr. Scott McIntyre, the cardiothoracic surgeon who sat across the conference room table from her. His familiar Mediterranean-Sea eyes were sympathetic, but his face remained somber.

The shock of seeing Scott again was only surpassed by the pain of his words. Her son was dying.

When had she slipped down the rabbit hole to this horror at Children's General Hospital? As if that weren't torment enough, she now faced a mother's worst nightmare, and the news was being delivered by Atlanta, Georgia's supposedly best cardiothoracic surgeon, a man who had hurt her badly years before.

In the movies this would have been called a twist of fate, horrible irony. But this wasn't some screenplay, this was her life. Her child, who always had a smile, her little boy, who giggled when she kissed him behind his ear, was in serious danger.

"He was doing fine. I was taking him for a scheduled check-up. Next thing I know his pediatrician has ordered an ambulance to bring us here." Hannah covered her mouth, damming the primal screams that threatened to escape. Moisture pooled in her eyes, blurring her vision of Scott...now Jake's doctor. "You have to be wrong."

He glanced at Andrea, the heart-transplant coordinator, sitting beside him, before he reached across the table as if to take Hannah's hand.

"Don't." She straightened. He withdrew.

That night eight years ago had started with a simple brush of his hand. She couldn't go there, wouldn't go there again, or she'd fall apart. She had to hold it together until her world righted itself. And it would, it had to. "I knew that a valve replacement might be in his future sooner than I had hoped, but a heart transplant? Your diagnosis can't be correct."

Scott ran a hand through his wavy hair. The soft, silky locks had gone from light to golden blond with age. His fingers threaded through his hair again, a mannerism Hannah remembered from when they'd been friends, good friends. They'd shared warm banter when he'd come to work on the step-down floor. The banter between them had developed into a friendship she'd valued, and had thought he had too.

Leaning forward, he brought her attention back to why they were sitting in this tiny, barren room, acting as if they'd never known each other intimately.

"I'm sorry, Hannah," he murmured with compassion. His voice strengthened with the words, "But the diagnosis *is* correct. The condition is called cardiomyopathy."

"Isn't that when the heart has become enlarged?" Hannah asked.

"Yes, it is. In Jake's case, he must have contracted a virus that went undetected. It settled on the valve he has had from birth—the one that wasn't working correctly. His heart is inflamed and is no longer pumping efficiently."

"He's had nothing more than a little runny nose. I assure you that if it had been more, I would've taken him to see a doctor."

"I'm not questioning your care for your son. The virus may have looked like something as simple as a cold, but it attacked his heart, damaging it. Sometimes it takes weeks to manifest itself and sometimes, like in Jake's case, only days or hours. There is no way to know how or when it will happen. But you would know that, being a nurse."

"Most of my work experience has been on an adult orthopedic floor and, anyway, I'm not nursing at present."

His head canted questioningly, but he said, "Still, you should understand the only thing we can do for your son—"

"His name is Jake." The words came out frosted. She wouldn't allow Jake to become a hospital number, just another patient in a bed.

Scott's gaze met hers. "Jake needs a new heart." His voice softened. "He needs to be listed right away."

Could she melt into the floor? Disappear? Maybe run so fast reality couldn't catch her?

"There has to be another way. Isn't there medication you can give him? I want a second opinion."

The skin around Scott lips tightened. He shook his head slightly, forestalling any further argument. "Hannah, you're welcome to get a second opinion. But we can't waste any time. Jake will die without the transplant. He might only have a few more weeks. The first thing we'll do is see that he is put on the United Network for Organ Sharing list."

She wiped away the dampness on her cheek. The framed pictures of the smiling children lining the walls of the tiny room mocked her. Her child should be one of them. Instead, he lay in a bed in the cardiac ICU, fighting for his life.

"I've examined Jake. He's stable for now. We're giving him anti-clotting drugs to prevent blood clots, which are common with cardiomyopathy, and watching for any arrhythmia."

Her eyes widened. "Blood clots! Arrhythmia!" She leaned toward him, hands gripping the edge of the table. "I want Jake listed now."

"Before we can do that, you'll need to have a psychological exam."

Her dazed look met his. "You have to be kidding. Jake is dying and you want me to have a psychological test? There's nothing wrong with me. It's your job to get Jake a heart, not see if my head's on straight."

Scott shifted in his chair, one of his long green scrubs-covered legs bumping against the table support. Despite being terrified by what he was telling her, Hannah couldn't help but compare the man in front of her with the one she had once known. A tall man years ago, his shoulders had broadened since she'd last seen him. Cute, in an all-American way then, now he was handsome as a man with power. Maturity and responsibility had added fine lines to his face, which she bet only made him more appealing to the nurses.

Scott still possessed the air of confidence that had made him the shining star of his medical class and the desire of the female personnel in the hospital. She, fortunately, had managed to remain immune to his playboy-to-the-core charm for a while, but not long enough.

"You need to calm down. Take a couple of deep breaths."

"Don't patronize me, Scott."

"Look, the visit to the psychologist is protocol. You'll be asked questions to make sure you understand what's involved with a transplant. The care afterwards is as important as the transplant itself. We need to know you can handle it."

She pushed back in her chair and crossed her arms over her chest. "I assure you I can take care of my son, both as a mother *and* as a nurse."

Propping his elbows on the table, Scott clasped his hands and used his index fingers to punctuate his words. "Hannah, I don't doubt it and I understand your frustration, but there are procedures."

At least he sounded as if he cared how she felt, unlike how he had acted years ago. Known for his excellent bedside manner then, in more ways than one, she'd never dreamed she'd ever be on the receiving end of his professional conduct.

"I have no interest in your procedures. I'm only interested in Jake getting well."

"If you really want that, you're going to have to work with me to see that it happens." His words had a razor-sharp edge, leaving her no room to argue.

"Okay then, I'm ready to do the interview." Hannah looked him directly in the eyes. "How much is all of this going to cost?"

He returned the same unwavering look. "Let's not worry about that. Keeping Jake healthy enough for the surgery is my primary concern."

Scott addressed Andrea. "Can you see that everything is set up for Han—uh…Mrs. Quinn's psychological?"

"I'll take care of it," Andrea responded.

Pushing the metal chair back, Scott stood. "I'll

speak to you again soon. I'm sorry this is happening to your son." He hesitated as if he wanted to say something further but thought better of it.

Wishing this situation would just go away, she gave Scott a tight smile.

"Andrea also has some forms that need to be filled out, so I'll leave you with her."

With that, Scott made a swift exit. She shouldn't be surprised he'd showed no more emotion. He'd done much the same thing the next morning after she'd made the mistake of succumbing to his charms. Their friendship had died, and so had her faith in him. Hannah let her brain shut down, and answered Andrea's questions by rote. When Andrea had finished, Hannah asked, "How good a surgeon is Scott, I mean Dr. McIntyre?"

"He's the best," Andrea stated, her voice full of assurance.

Was she just another woman who had fallen under Scott's spell and could sing nothing but his praises? "I can't let Jake die."

"Mrs. Quinn." Andrea placed her hand on Hannah's arm. "Dr. McIntyre is a brilliant surgeon. He'll take excellent care of your son. You can trust him."

Andrea guided Hannah to the waiting room and

to an area away from the other parents. Hannah sank onto a blue vinyl sofa and put her head in her hands, letting pent-up tears flow. She understood what she'd been told, but she wasn't entirely convinced. Hannah couldn't afford to be blindly accepting where her son's care was concerned. He was all she had.

Hannah studied the blue square pattern of the carpet. She had no idea that Andrea had sat down beside her until she laid a comforting hand on Hannah's shoulder.

Andrea said, "You'll get through this. Why don't you go back and see Jake? Visiting hours will be over soon."

Entering the cardiac unit, Hannah checked in with the clerk at the large circular desk situated in the middle of an enormous open room. Of the twenty or so beds around the wall, only one interested her, the third one on the left, where her little boy lay so still.

Her precious child looked small and pale stretched out on the white sheet of the big bed. Wires ran from him to the surrounding machines. She'd seen this before, during nursing training, but this time it was *her* child lying there.

It's just you and me, honey. Don't leave me. Jake's usually sparkling blue eyes were clouded with fear as they pleaded for reassurance. Hannah took his tiny hand in hers, careful not to touch any of the IV lines. Her chest tightened. She placed a kiss on his forehead before stroking his dark baby curls while making a soft cooing sound that settled him.

"Mrs. Quinn?" A young woman stepped to the foot of the bed. I'll be Jake's nurse for today. You may come back to visit any time during the day but you need to call first and get permission."

What if something happens while I'm not here? Could I live with myself if it did? Would I want to? Her hands shook, and her stomach jumped. Wrapping her arms around her waist, she squeezed. "Can I stay with him tonight?"

She sensed instead of saw Scott step beside her.

"I'm afraid not." His words would've been harsh except they were said in such a low, gentle tone that they came out sounding compassionate, regretful.

"I don't see why not. I'm a nurse."

"But as Jake's mother you need to take care of yourself. Rest. Leave a number with the nurse and she'll call if you're needed." He gave Jake's nurse an appreciative smile.

The fresh-out-of-nursing-school girl blinked twice before she said in a syrupy tone, "I'll put it on his chart, Dr. McIntyre."

"I don't see—" Hannah began.

"Those are the rules. You have to be out of here by seven and can't come back in until eight in the morning," Scott said in a flat, authoritative tone.

"I guess I don't have a choice, then."

"No, you don't." Scott's words came out even and to the point.

Enunciating the numbers to her cellphone with care, Hannah watched to make sure each one was written correctly. The way the nurse was acting around Scott, she might make a mistake.

As Hannah gave the last digit Scott approached his patient's bed. "Hello, Jake. I'm Dr. McIntyre. You can call me Dr. Mac."

Jake didn't look at Scott's face, but focused instead on his chest, reaching his hand out.

Hannah moved around the bed to stand opposite Scott to see what Jake was so engrossed in.

"Oh, I see you found my friend." Scott smiled down at Jake. "His name is Bear. He rides around with me. Would you like to hold him?"

Jake's eyes lost their look of fear as they remained riveted on the tiny animal. His fingers wiggled in an effort to reach the toy.

Unclipping the toy from his stethoscope, Scott offered it to Jake.

Scott's charm obviously extended to his young patients. Jake didn't always take to new people but Scott had managed to make her son grin despite the ugliness of the place. Hannah sighed. Scott looked up and gave her a reassuring smile. She didn't like the stream of warmth that flowed through her cold body. Still, a kind, familiar face in her life was reassuring right now, even if it was Scott's.

"My bear hasn't been well. Could he stay with you?" Jake gave Scott a weak nod before Scott handed Jake the bear. "I need to listen to your heart now. I'm going to put this little thing on you and the other end in my ears, okay?"

Small creases of concentration formed between Scott's eyes as he moved the instrument across Jake's outwardly perfect chest. She'd always admired Scott's strong, capable hands. The same ones that were caring for her child had skimmed across her body with equal skill and confidence. She shivered. Those memories should've been long buried, covered over with bitter disappointment.

She'd been around enough doctors to recognize one secure in his abilities. Scott seemed to have stepped into the role of pediatric surgeon with no effort. He certainly knew what to do to keep Jake from being scared, at least she'd give him that much. Maybe she could put her hope in him professionally, if not emotionally. She wanted to trust him. Desperately wanted to.

Jake's eyelids drooped but he continued to clutch the toy.

Scott removed the earpieces, looping the stethoscope around his neck.

"Scott, thanks for giving Jake the bear. He looked so afraid before. I still can't believe he needs a heart transplant," she said in little more than a whisper that held all the agony she felt. "He doesn't look that sick."

She prayed his next words would contradict the truth she saw on his face.

"I realize that by looking at him it's hard to believe, but it is the truth."

Hannah's knees shook. With swift agility, Scott circled the bed, his fingers wrapping her waist, steadying her.

She jerked away. The warmth of his touch radiated through her.

As if conscious of the nurse nearby, he dropped his hand to his side.

"I'm fine." For a second she'd wanted to lean against him, to take the support he offered.

Hannah peered at him. Had hurt filled his eyes before they'd turned businesslike again? The unexpected look had come and gone with the flicker of his lids. Had she really seen it? Could she trust herself to interpret his looks correctly?

"You need to understand a heart transplant isn't a fix. It's exchanging one set of problems for another. Jake will always be on meds and have to come to the hospital for regular check-ups."

"I understand that. I'll take care of him."

Scott placed a reassuring hand on her shoulder.

"Don't touch me."

He dropped his hand. "Hannah, I know this is rough. But we were friends at one time. Please let me help."

"Look, Scott, the only help I need from you is to get Jake a heart."

"Hannah, we're going to get Jake through this."

"I hope so. My son's life depends on you." She

couldn't afford for him to be wrong, the stakes were much too high.

"Hannah, with a heart transplant Jake can live."

Like before? Would he still squeal when she blew on his belly? Would he giggle when she blew bubbles and they burst above his head? Her sweet, loving child was dying in front of her eyes.

Scott was saying all the right things, but could she believe him? "It's not your kid, so you really don't have any idea how hard this is, do you?"

The muscle in his jaw jumped, before he said, "No, I guess I don't. But I do know I'm a skilled surgeon and this is an excellent hospital with outstanding staff. We can help Jake and we will."

"I'm counting on that."

In his office, using the time between surgeries, Scott waded through the stack of papers cluttering his desk. He leaned back in his chair. Hannah's face with those expressive green eyes slipped into his mind for the hundredth—or was it the thousandth?—time in the last few hours. She'd looked just as shocked to see him as he'd been to see her. It had required all his concentration to stay focused on what they had been discussing.

He couldn't have been more astonished to find a red-eyed Hannah looking at him expectantly as he'd entered the conference room. Andrea normally arrived ahead of him but she'd had to answer a page. He'd stepped into the room, and back through time.

Hannah's hushed whisper of his name had made him want to hug her. But she'd made it clear she'd never allow him. Guilt washed over him. Of course she didn't want his comfort. He'd hurt her, and for that he was sorry, but he'd believed it was for the best.

He'd wanted her desperately that night eight years ago, and she'd come to him so sweet and willingly, trust filling her eyes. If he could have stopped, he would have, but, heaven help him, he hadn't been able to. He'd handled things poorly the next morning. She had been too young, in her second year of nursing school. He had been an intern with a career plan that wouldn't allow him to be distracted. He'd refused to lead her on, have her make plans around him. He hadn't been ready to commit then, and he wouldn't commit now.

Andrea had entered before he'd let his emotions get out of control. Regret had washed over him, for not only what he had to tell Hannah but for what life would be like with a sick child and for their lost friendship.

Based on her reaction today, he'd killed whatever had been between them. She'd not been cool to him, she'd been dead-of-winter-in-Alaska cold toward him. Compared to the way she used to treat everyone when they'd worked together, almost hostile.

Not the type of woman that made men do a double-take, Hannah still had an innate appeal about her. He'd known it back then and, even while telling her the devastating news of her son, that connection between them was still there.

Speaking to any parent about their deathly ill child was difficult. Sending a child home with smiling parents after a life-giving transplant made it all worthwhile. Scott's intention was to put such a smile of happiness on Hannah's face.

Scott shook his head as if to dislodge Hannah from his mind. He let his chair drop forward, and picked up an envelope off the stack of mail on his desk. The familiar sunshine emblem of the Medical Hospital for Children in Dallas, Texas, stood out in the return spot. A surge of anticipation filled him as he opened it. Was this the news he'd been hoping for?

A quick tap came at the door and Andrea entered.

The statuesque, older nurse had worked with way too many young surgeons to be overly impressed by him when he'd arrived at Children's General. Still, she'd had pity on him and had taken him under her wing, helping him when he'd needed to navigate the ins and outs of hospital politics. They had become fast friends.

"Is that the news you've been looking for?" Andrea indicated the letter.

He'd been talking to the administrator at MHC for months about starting a heart-transplant program there. He opened the flap and pulled out the letter. "Not quite. They're still looking at other candidates. They'll let me know of their decision soon."

"You're still top man on their list, aren't you?" Andrea asked.

"Yeah, but they want to review a few more of my cases." He'd geared his entire career toward this opportunity. To set up his own program, train a team, and make the program in Dallas the best in the country.

"Don't worry, boss. I'm sure they're impressed with your skills."

With years of experience as an OR nurse, Andrea didn't look like she had a soft touch, but she had a talent for making parents feel comfortable. That was a gift he valued. Appreciative of the skills she brought to her job, Scott intended to persuade her to become a part of his new team in Dallas if he was offered the position.

"Thanks for the vote of confidence."

"I've got the latest blood work on the Quinn kid. You wanted it ASAP."

Scott took the lab sheet and studied it. "We shouldn't have a problem listing him right away."

"None that I can think of." With a purse of her lips and a glint of questioning in her eye, Andrea said, "I know I came into the meeting late, but I've never known you to call a parent by their first name. So I'm assuming you two know each other."

"Yes, we met while I was in med school, just before I left for my surgical training." Meeting her look, he refused to give any more information.

Andrea raised her brows. "Oh. Interesting spot you're in, Doc. She didn't sound particularly happy to see you again. History coming back to bite you?"

Few others would've gotten away with such an insubordinate question.

At his huff, she grinned and slipped back out the door.

Scott might have found some absurd humor in the situation if it wasn't such a serious one, and if he hadn't been so afraid that Andrea was right.

Hannah was the one nurse that had mattered, too much. The one that had gotten under his skin, making him wish for more. He'd pushed her away because she'd deserved better than he'd been able to give. He still couldn't believe Hannah had re-entered his life and, of all things, as the mother of one of his patients. Life took funny bends and turns and this had to be one of the most bizarre he'd ever experienced.

But it didn't matter what their relationship had been or was now. What mattered was that her son got his second chance at life.

Hannah made her way to the snack machine area on the bottom floor during the afternoon shift change. She was sitting in a booth, dunking her bag in the steaming water, when Scott walked up.

Her breath caught. He was still the most handsome man she'd ever known. His strong jaw line and generous mouth gave him a youthful appearance that contrasted sharply with the experienced surgeon he surely was. There was nothing old or distinguished about him, not even a gray hair to indicate his age.

He still wore the Kelly-green scrubs covered by a pristine white lab coat, which meant he'd been in surgery. She couldn't see the writing on the left side of his coat, but she knew what was printed above the pocket.

Embroidered in navy was "Scott T. McIntyre, MD" and under that was "Department of Thoracic Surgery." Reading those words over and over during their meeting had been her attempt to disconnect from the surreal turn her life had taken. She'd almost reached across the small table and traced the letters with a finger. He'd gotten what he'd wanted. She couldn't help but be proud for him.

Scott stepped to the coffee-dispensing machine and dug into his pocket. Pulling his hand out, he looked at his open palm, muttered something under his breath and spilled the coins back into his pants.

"Here." She offered him some quarters in her outstretched hand.

Blinking in surprise, he turned. "Hey. I didn't see you sitting there."

"I know. You were miles away."

With a wry smile, he accepted the change. His fingertips tickled the soft skin of her palm as he took the money.

A zip of electricity ran up her arm. It was a familiar, pleasant feeling, one that her body remembered. But her mind said not to. She put her hand under the table, rubbing it against her jeans-clad leg in an effort to ease the sensation.

Scott purchased his coffee then glanced at her, as if unsure what to do next. She couldn't remember seeing him anything but confident. He appeared as off-kilter as she.

He hesitated. "Do you mind if I join you?"

"You know, Scott, I'm not really up to rehashing the past right now."

"I really think we should talk."

Hannah took a second to respond. Could she take any more emotional upheaval especially when she'd just started believing she could breathe again after their last meeting?

Her "Okay" came out sounding unwelcoming.

One of his long legs brushed her knee as he slid into the booth. That electric charge sparked again. She drew her legs deeper into the space beneath the table.

"I've just seen the psychologist. Is Jake listed?" Hannah asked into the tense silence hovering between them.

"I put him on a few minutes ago." Scott's tone implied it was no big deal, an everyday occurrence, which it might be for him. For her, it was a major event.

She breathed a sigh of relief.

Scott sipped his coffee, before setting the paper cup on the table. He looked at her. "I have to ask: where is Mr. Quinn?"

"That's not really your business, is it?"

"Yes, and no. If he's going to be coming into the hospital and making parental demands and disrupting Jake's care, yes, it is. For the other, I'm just curious."

"There's no worries where he's concerned." Her look bored into his. "He left us."

Scott's flinch was barely discernible. "When?"

"Just after Jake was born."

"You've no family?"

"None nearby. My sister is living in California

now. I told her to hold off coming. I don't know how long we'll have to wait on a heart."

His sympathetic regard made her look away. "There's no one that can be here with you?"

"No. When you're a single parent with a small child, relatively new to town and you have to work, it leaves little time to make friends."

"I understand. Doctors' hours are much the same way."

"As I remember it, you didn't have any trouble making time for a social life." She softened the dig with a wry curl of her lips.

He chuckled. That low, rough sound vibrated around them and through her.

She took a sip of her tea.

Scott drained his cup before looking at her again. "Uh, Hannah, about us…"

"There *is* no us."

"You know what I mean. You have to admit this situation is unusual at best."

She placed her cup on the table. "Scott, the only thing I'm interested in is Jake getting a new heart. Whatever we had or didn't have was over and done with years ago. You're Jake's heart surgeon. That's our only relationship." She probably sounded bitter, but she didn't have the energy to deal with her emotions where he was concerned. Particularly not today. She needed time to think, to sort through her feelings. Scott twisted his coffee cup around, making a tapping noise on the table.

"Hannah, I shouldn't have left like I did. I thought I was doing the best thing for you. I was wrong not to tell you I was leaving town."

She put up her hands. "Let's just concentrate on Jake. I don't have the energy to rehash the past."

He gave a resigned nod, but she didn't think the subject permanently closed.

"Then would you at least tell me why you're not nursing?"

"I took a leave of absence when Jake started getting sicker. I didn't think he needed to be in a day-care situation, and I couldn't find private care close enough to home to make it work."

"That's understandable. I thought you had quit altogether. I remember how much you enjoyed it. What a good nurse you were…are."

"Yeah, I still love it. I'll get back to it when Jake's better."

He'd made no attempt to be a part of her life in the last eight years, and now he was interested in her personal life? Picking up a napkin on the table, she wadded it into a ball.

Hoping to avoid further questions, she asked, "How about you? Where did you go…uh…for your surgery residency?" She'd almost said "after you left me alone in bed. Without saying a word."

He pulled his legs out from under the table, extended them across the floor, and crossed one ankle over the other.

"Texas, then to Boston for a while. I took a position here a couple of years ago."

"You always said you wanted to be a heart surgeon. You didn't change your mind."

"No. After hearing my first baby's irregular heartbeat during my cardio rotation I've been set on it. It took me years to qualify, but it was the right move." His gaze met hers. "But it meant making some tough decisions."

"So, is there a Mrs. McIntyre and any little McIntyres?"

Hannah held her breath, waiting for his answer. A part of her wished he'd found no one special, while another part wanted him to be happy.

"There's no Mrs. McIntyre or children."

Hannah released the breath she'd held. Why'd she feel such a sense of relief? "Why's that?"

"A surgeon's life doesn't lend itself to a peaceful private life. Somehow my patients always take precedence over anything or anyone else."

A dark shadow crossed his face that she didn't quite comprehend. Had he almost married? What had happened?

"As the mother of one of your patients I'm grateful you make them a priority. I believe that would be a part of being a great doctor. " She took a sip of tea. "So, are you still seeing a nurse on every floor and in every department?" The question had a sting to it that she couldn't help but add.

He chuckled. "You don't have a very high opinion of me, do you?"

Hannah chose to let that question remain unanswered. "Did you know that the joke in the nurses' station was that, when you had rotated to our floor, you'd asked for an alphabetical listing of all the single nurses and were working your way through the list?"

"I did not."

"What? Know or ask for the list? Because you sure as heck worked your way through the staff. I watched you. With the last name of Watson, I had time to see you coming." Heavens, she'd gotten what she'd deserved. She'd seen for herself what a player he had been.

"Yeah, and you refused to play along. That was one of the many things I liked about you. You made me work to get your attention."

"I wasn't interested in being another nurse you scratched off your list."

Scott's hand covered his heart. "Ouch, that hurt."

She grinned. "That might have been too harsh."

He smiled, oozing Dr. McDreamy charm. "Same Hannah. You never cut me any slack. But as it turns out, believe it or not, being a surgeon doesn't leave me as much free time as being a med student did. As for an answer, I hope I've grown up some."

"I know I have. I understand things I didn't use to." Like how it felt to be drawn to the bright fire that was his charisma and get burnt. He was speaking as if they'd shared nothing more than a casual meal all those years ago, instead of a friendship that had ended with a night filled with passion. She had repeated the same mistake with Jake's dad.

"I'm sorry, Hannah, for everything." His beeper went off, demanding his attention. "I have to see about this. Thanks for the coffee." He picked up his cup, crushed it and pitched it into the nearest trash can.

Scott moved down the hall as if he was a man in command, a man on a mission. He'd been intense and focused as a medical student. That didn't seem to have changed, but he also had the ability to laugh and smile effortlessly, which drew people to him.

Taking a deep breath, she slowly released it. She needed to think. Put things in some order in her mind.

Jake. Heart transplant. Waiting. Cost. Die. Scott. The words ping-ponged off the walls of her mind.

CHAPTER TWO

SCOTT peered over the unit desk toward Hannah, who sat at her son's bed. Her head had fallen to one side against the back cushion of the chair. Even with the burden of worry showing on her features, she caught and held his attention. Her chestnut-colored hair brushed the tops of her shoulders and hung forward, curtaining one cheek. If he'd been standing closer, he would've pushed it back.

Puffy eyes and stricken looks were so much a part of his profession that he had become impervious to them, but telling Hannah about Jake's heart condition had been the toughest thing he'd ever done. She was no longer the impressionable nursing student he'd once known. Hannah was now a mother warrior fighting for her child. He believed her strength and spirit would see her through.

She'd made it clear that their only association

would be a professional one. He could be there for her as a friend, for old times' sake. The only sensible choice was to keep their relationship a professional one. Being involved with a parent on a personal level was a huge ethical no-no anyway. Lawyers didn't represent family members, and surgeons didn't treat loved ones, or, in his case, family.

Hannah shifted in the chair and shoved her tresses out of her face. She looked tired, worn and dejected. She stirred, causing her hair to fall further across her face. With effort, Scott resisted the urge to go to her, take her in his arms and whisper that everything would be all right. She'd always brought out the protective side of him. She'd never believe it but he'd left her that morning all those years ago in order to protect her. Even then medicine had been his all-consuming focus. He'd gotten that trait from his father.

As a small-town doctor, his father had been on call day and night. Scott had watched him leave the supper table numerous times to see a sick child after eating only one forkful of food. More than once Scott had heard him return to the house in the early hours of the morning after seeing a patient. Their family had even returned early from a vacation because an elderly woman his father had been treating had taken a turn for the worse and was asking for him. Scott had never once heard his father complain. All Scott had ever wanted was to be like his father. He had thought he was the finest doctor he'd ever known.

Hannah woke with a start, blinking fast. Daylight had turned to darkness outside the window but the fluorescent lighting made it bright in the room. She straightened.

"Mommy."

She hopped up and went to Jake's bedside.

"Hi, sweetheart. We both had a little nap." She brushed his hair back from his forehead. "How you doing?" She kissed him.

The nurse pushed medicine into the port of the IV located at the side of Jake's tiny wrist. Giving the IV set-up a critical look, Hannah realized old habits did die hard. She still wished she could take a more active role in Jake's care. As long as he was in CICU she had to remain on the sideline.

"Would you like to hold him for a while?" the nurse asked as she punched buttons on the IV pump and it responded with small beeps.

Moisture filled her eyes. "Could I, please?"

"Sure. You have a seat in the chair and I'll help you get him situated."

After a little maneuvering of IV lines and moving of machines, Hannah had Jake in her arms. It was pure heaven.

"Go home," Jake mumbled as he settled against her.

"I wish we could, but hopefully you won't be here long."

She looked over Jake's head at the nurse as he played with his toy bear.

The nurse spoke softly, "You know, Mrs. Quinn, I've seen some very sick kids come through here who are doing great after having a transplant."

The words reassured Hannah somewhat. At least she was getting to hold him. That more than satisfied her for the time being.

"If you don't mind, while he's sitting with you I'm going to step over to the next bed and help another nurse with her patient. Will you be okay?"

"Sure." Hannah's gaze shifted to Jake again. He looked like a small cherub. His lips were getting bluer, though. She had to admit Scott was right. Jake needed a heart. *Soon.*

She put her cheek against Jake's. "I love you."

"I luv 'oo."

Moisture filled her eyes. *Loving...was...hard.*

Her head jerked up at the sharp insistent beeps of the monitor that turned into an alarm. Staff rushed into Jake's cubicle. Scott came with them. "Hannah, let me have Jake." Scott took Jake from her and laid him on the bed, all the while issuing orders.

Hannah stepped to the bed. Her hands gripped the rail. "What's wrong?" she whispered, fear coiling in her middle.

Scott looked at her as he listened to Jake's chest. "Hannah, you need to leave." His authoritarian tone told her he'd accept no argument. His attention immediately returned to Jake.

She was a nurse, Jake was her son. *She could help.*

But as much as she wanted to stay, Hannah knew he was right. She'd been involved in enough emergencies to know that the fewer people around the bed the better. If she wasn't allowed to assist then she would be in the way. Slowly, she stepped back.

Scott's gaze caught hers. "I'll be out to talk to you when Jake is stable."

Hannah walked toward the doors but took one

final look over her shoulder as she left the unit. Jake's bed was no longer visible because of the number of people surrounding it.

Finding one of the small conference rooms off the hallway empty and dark, she stepped inside, not bothering with the light. Her eyes ached from the dry air and the bright lights. She dropped onto one of the chairs situated as far from the door as possible.

Unable to control her anguish any longer, Hannah's dam broke and her soft crying turned into sobs.

Now that Jake was resting comfortably, Scott needed to find Hannah. He paused in the hall.

What was that sound? There it was again. It was coming from the consultation room. He stepped closer to the entrance. Dark inside, no one should be in there. Was that someone crying?

He couldn't ignore it. In a hospital it wasn't unusual to hear crying, but this sounded like someone in physical pain.

With tentative steps, he entered the room. "Hello?"

A muffled sob filled the space.

"Are you okay?"

"I'm fine. Please go away." The words were little more than a whisper coming from the corner, followed by a sniff.

Even when it was full of sorrow, he recognized her voice. *Hannah.* The stricken look on her face when he'd ordered her to leave still troubled him. He'd been surprised she hadn't put up more of a fight.

"Hannah?"

A whimper answered, then a muffled "Please leave" came from the corner. Moving into the room, he gave his eyes time to adjust to the dim light spilling in from the hallway. Scott had seen patients in pain, but her agony reached deep within him. Hearing Hannah sobbing knocked the breath out of him. It was killing him to stand behind professionally closed doors where she was concerned.

But if he did open that metaphorical door, would he be able to step through? Could he help her? Did he have the right to get involved so deeply in her life? What he did know with unshaking certainty was that he couldn't walk away. He couldn't make the same mistake twice. The consequences could be too great.

Coming toward her, Scott lowered his voice.

"It's Scott. Hannah, honey, Jake is fine. He had a reaction to the new med. He's all right now."

Her head rose enough that he could see her eyes over the ridge of her arm. The rest of her face remained covered.

"Go. Away." The words were sharp and wrapped in pure misery. She turned her back to him and lowered her head again. "I don't need you."

Those words stung. Scott touched her and she flinched. He removed his hand. It wounded him that she wouldn't accept his help. Was she really that untrusting of him? "He's resting now, really."

Scott sank into the chair beside hers. He'd dealt with parents besieged by strong feelings. It was part of his job, but Hannah's pain reached deep to a spot he kept closed off. A place he shouldn't go with the parent of a patient, especially not with her. Somewhere he wasn't comfortable or confident in going.

Then again, his failure to recognize how distressed his mother had been when his parents had divorced had had disastrous results. He'd promised himself then to never let that happen again to someone he cared about. He wasn't leaving Hannah, no matter what she said or how she acted. Her obvious pain went too deep to dismiss.

Hannah made a slight shift in her seat toward him, then said in a hard voice, "I don't—want you here. Go away and leave me alone."

She was in so much pain she was contradicting herself. He could resist a lot, but Hannah's pain brought down the final wall. He had to do something, at least try.

A feeling of inadequacy washed over him. What could he say to make it better? Could he help her? Scott placed a hand on her shoulder, feeling the inflexible muscles. As if she were a troubled child, he began moving his hand in comforting circles along her back.

"Scott, stop." She twisted her shoulders back and forth, but he refused to let her have her way. He may not have the correct words or be able to change the situation but he could hold her, be there to comfort her.

"Hannah, I'm not leaving."

She stilled.

"Look, you're a fighter. And if Jake is anything like you, he is too."

He wrapped an arm around her shoulders and pulled her to him. She stiffened and pushed against his chest. "Let me help you get through this." His grip tightened and he tucked her head under his chin. Holding her as close as the chairs would allow, he said in a tender voice, "Let me be your friend. You need someone."

She remained rigid, but he refused to ease his hold. Taking several halting breaths, she gave up the battle and relaxed against him.

Hannah's distress was difficult to witness. He didn't flinch when he opened a child's chest or when making life-and-death decisions but he couldn't stand seeing Hannah in so much pain. He wanted to make it go away, make it his own.

"Why won't you leave me alone?" she murmured against his chest.

"You need to be held, and I'm going to do that. Cry all you want. I'll be right here when you're ready to talk."

Having her in his arms went beyond wonderful, even with her crying and heartbroken. It felt right. He'd not only stepped over the invisible don't-get-personally-involved line, he'd jumped. But he'd see to it remained one friend comforting another. He wouldn't, couldn't, let it become personal.

Holding her firmly against him, he made calm reassuring noises that made little sense. With his voice low, he spoke to her as if she were a hurt animal. After a few minutes she quieted. Pure satisfaction coursed through him like brandy on a cold night.

He placed a fleeting kiss to her forehead, which smelt like fresh apples. She still used the same shampoo. With his cheek resting against her hair, he took a deep breath, letting her scent fill him.

Neither spoke. Her breathing gradually became even and regular. The sensation of her body pressed against his made his thoughts travel back to what could have been. Was he taking advantage of her vulnerability? Yeah, but he still couldn't resist resting his lips against her skin again.

Scott comprehended for the first time in his life what it meant to want to carry someone else's burden. He longed to take Hannah's hurt away. Fix her problems. Yet he could never be her knight. His duty to others would always be pulling him off the horse.

With a sigh of resignation, she completely relaxed against his chest. She had to be drained in both body and mind.

Having Hannah in his arms brought back memories of that night. Even then he couldn't help but touch her, hold her. Now she needed to be held, desperately, and he was afraid that he needed the contact just as much. Everything about Hannah pushed his common sense away.

Heavens. She was being held by Scott.

"Better?" he asked.

In a quick movement Hannah straightened and shifted back into her chair. She should've never let him touch her. Mercy, it had felt wonderful. She was so tired of being alone, carrying the load for Jake's care. At least with Scott she had a partner until the transplant was done.

Under Scott's scrutiny, she refused to meet his gaze. "I've never fallen apart like that before," she muttered.

"Are you positive you're okay?" He sounded as unsure as she felt.

"I'm better now," she said, though her words lacked confidence. "You can go."

"Have you eaten today?"

Why wouldn't he leave her alone? She closed her eyes, then lifted them, looking through her lashes. "If I answer you, will you leave?" She didn't want to have a reason to start caring for him again.

Scott said nothing but gave her a hard look.

"Okay, I had a bowl of cereal this morning. I was going to eat during shift change…" she sighed "…but I just wasn't hungry. Satisfied?" Where was the ever ever-present sound of his pager going off when she needed it?

He shook his head. "You're one of the most intelligent women I know so I expected better from you. What did I tell you about taking care of yourself?"

"I heard you."

"But you don't plan to follow orders." Cynicism wrapped his words.

She straightened her shoulders. "I don't have to follow your orders. You're Jake's doctor, not mine." At his chuckle, she realized he'd baited her on purpose to make her show some kind of animation.

"That might be, but if you'd followed my orders…" He cocked his head to the side in question.

"It must feel good to be a know-it-all."

"It does have its advantages. Let's go get a bite to eat."

"Us?"

"Yeah, us. I eat too. I certainly can't trust you to see to feeding yourself. Anyway, I like to share a meal with someone when I can. I eat too many dinners alone."

"That's hard to believe. You can't find a nurse to eat with?" She'd never known him to have trouble getting dinner dates. Had he really changed that much?

"I did. You."

She huffed. "You know what I mean."

"I do, but I'm pretending I don't. Come on. Keep me company."

"I don't really want to go, but you're not going to give up until I agree, are you?"

He grinned and shook his head.

She'd consider it payment for him giving her a shoulder to cry on. And she was just too tired, too scared and too emotionally drained to fight him off. Besides, having one meal with Scott wouldn't change anything between them.

After a long moment she nodded her agreement. "But I'm going to check on Jake first."

"I never thought any different." He took her elbow and helped her stand. The pad of his thumb skimmed across the bare skin of her forearm. She shivered and stepped away.

Tugging at the hem of her pink T-shirt, she said, "I'm fine now."

He remained close as they moved toward the door. Her head seemed to be on straight again, but having Scott so near was making her nerves fire in double time.

What was happening? She'd given up acting like a schoolgirl long ago. Given up on him. She hadn't needed anyone in a long time, but she'd fallen apart in Scott's arms. Hannah shook her head to remove lingering feelings of being cherished while in Scott's embrace. Years ago he'd acted as if he cared, and she'd been crushed. She wouldn't let it happen again.

Jake was sitting up in the bed, playing with the toy that Scott had given him, when they walked into his cubicle.

"Mommy." He reached his hand over the rail of his bed.

She took his little hand in hers and placed a quick kiss on the top of it. "Hi, sweetie."

"Hello, Jake," Scott said, as he move around to the other side of the bed from Hannah. "While you're talking to your mom, I'm going to give you a little check. It won't hurt, I promise."

Scott slipped two fingers around Jake's wrist, feeling for his pulse before he stepped to the end of the bed. Pulling the blanket back, Scott placed the tips of two fingers on the top of Jake's foot to check his *dorsalis pedis* pulse.

At Scott's finger skimmed Jake's skin, her little boy jerked his foot away.

Scott looked up at Jake and smiled. "Do you like to be tickled?"

Jake nodded.

Cupping Jake's heel, Scott ran a finger down the bottom of Jake's foot. Her son laughed. Scott's low rumble of mirth joined Jake's.

Hannah couldn't help but smile. Her heart lightened. For the first time all day she believed Jake might get well.

Her laugh drew both males' attention as if they'd forgotten she was even there.

The overhead lights dimmed.

"It's time for your mom and me to let you sleep," Scott said to Jake as he pulled the blanket back over the tiny foot.

Hannah squeezed Jake's hand and kissed him on the forehead. "I love you, honey."

Scott nodded to a nurse standing behind her, who she'd not noticed until then. The nurse inserted a needle into Jake's IV port and emptied the syringe's contents.

"That should help him sleep," Scott said as he

came to stand beside Hannah. "He'll have a comfortable night, so don't worry."

"Yeah, that's easier said than done." Hannah watched Jake's eyelids droop. When she felt his hand go limp, she placed it on the bed. Pulling the blue hospital blanket up, she tucked Jake in.

The urge to scoop Jake up and take him home to his own bed had never been stronger.

"Come, Hannah," Scott said in a sympathetic voice. "It's time to see about yourself. You need to eat."

As they waited for the elevator to go down to the cafeteria, Scott kept glancing at her. He'd been wonderful with Jake, but he was making her nervous now. Did Scott think she was going to fall into his bed again just because he'd made her son giggle?

She curled her hands together and intertwined her fingers again.

As close as they'd been at one time, they were little more than strangers now. She'd changed, was a mother now, and had been a wife. Maybe Scott had changed too. Relief flowed through her as the elevator doors slid open. Hannah stepped in and stood in a corner. She was glad that Scott chose to stand on the opposite side.

The jerk of the elevator as they dropped to the bottom floor made her grab the rail on the wall.

Scott moved nearer. "Are you okay?"

"Yes."

His gaze met hers then moved to her lips and lingered.

Her mouth went hot-summer dry. Her head spun. Had someone turned off the air-conditioning?

The elevator stopped and the doors slid open. Scott's eyes lifted. A smoldering look filled them. Hannah blinked. Gathering her wits, she slipped by him. As she exited, his warm breath ruffled her hair against her cheek.

He followed. "Let's go to the cafeteria instead of the snack machines. Wednesday is fried chicken day, the best thing they make."

Scott spoke as if the intense moment in the elevator had never occurred. Had having her back in his life affected him at all? Perhaps it hadn't.

"I think I'll just have a BLT and a cup of hot tea," Hannah said.

"I'm going for the chicken. Find us a table. Tell Lucy at the register that I'll pay for yours when I come through."

"I won't let you do that," she said as she stepped toward the grill line. "This isn't a date."

He held up his hand and grinned. "Okay, okay."

His boyish smile made her feel like she was sitting in the sun on a spring day, pure bliss. Her heart fluttered. He still had that devastating effect on her.

Don't stare. *Think.*

Hannah forced herself to turn around and go to the sandwich line. The mundane business of selecting a sandwich and the physical distance from Scott helped to settle her nerves. She'd moved into the register line when Scott came up behind her. Bending down, he said, "I'm getting yours."

He was too close. She was too conscious of him. He paid before she could form a protest.

Outside the high arched windows a slow, steady rain began to fall. The water on the concrete walk shimmered in the glow from the security light. The weather reflected her life. Dark, with hints of brightness.

Moving toward the dining area, she selected a table in the center of the room, if only to put a physical object between them as a way to regain her equilibrium. Scott glanced at an available booth and shrugged. His mouth lifted into the beginning of a grin before he took the chair opposite hers.

Hannah concentrated on keeping the bacon between the pieces of toast while Scott ate his fried chicken. It amazed her that after the heated moments earlier they could still manage a comfortable silence between them. They'd slipped back into that easy place they'd enjoyed when he'd been in medical school.

Cleaning his plate, Scott sat back with a sigh, giving her a quizzical look. "Feel better now you've had some food?"

Her heart skipped a beat. He'd caught her staring. "Yes, much. But I do insist on paying for my meal."

"I owed you for coffee. Anyway, can't two old friends eat together without fighting over the bill?"

"We're just acquaintances." She fiddled with her glass a second before pinning him with a look. "True friends don't leave without saying a word."

His lips formed a tight line before he said, "Hannah, I realize you're still angry with me and I don't blame you."

She opened her mouth to speak.

"No, please hear me out. I know you don't want to go into the past. I appreciate that. You're having a rough time and I'd like to help if you'll let me." He laid a hand over hers, blanketing it.

Her heart thumped faster. She didn't know how to force her body to be sensible where Scott was concerned.

It would be nice to have someone to lean on. It was tempting to accept his offer, for at least a little while, until she could right her world long enough to think straight. But could Scott be that person, with their past looming between them?

And he was Jake's doctor.

"I guess we can try." They'd been friends before, maybe they could be again. She was just too exhausted in spirit and mind to argue. "But you'll have to earn my friendship and that will be *all* there is between us. Friendship." She tugged her hand from beneath his.

The stiffness in his body eased and, with a gentle smile, he said, "I understand."

With one finger, Hannah circled the salt shaker sitting in the middle of the table. She rolled it from side to side. The base of the glass knocked against the wood.

Scott took the shaker, setting it aside. "I wish

I could make the situation with Jake easier for you."

"I appreciate that." She gave him a weary smile. "I hate not being able to help care for him. I am his mother and a nurse."

Scott opened his mouth to speak, but she forestalled him.

"I know. Protocol. I understand it, but don't like it."

He laughed softly. "And I understand where you're coming from. I know that right now it seems like all you're doing is sitting around, watching and waiting, but once Jake goes to the floor I promise you there'll be plenty to do. Plenty to learn."

"I hope I don't sound too whiny. I've been Jake's sole parent for so long it's hard to relinquish control. I understand why I'm not allowed to do more but that doesn't mean my heart accepts it."

He nodded. "So, do you plan to return to the same position when Jake recovers, or do you want to work elsewhere? Maybe a satellite clinic?"

Hannah leaned back against the chair, pulling her lower lip between her teeth. "I hadn't thought about doing that. Working at a clinic isn't a bad idea. The hours are better, and it may be easier to arrange care for Jake if I did." She sat up again, crossing her arms and leaned on the table. "Have I satisfied all your questions?"

"No, but I'll save some for another time." Downing the rest of his drink, he asked, "Are you ready to go? I've an early morning and you've had a hard day. We both need to get to bed."

At her surprised look he realized what he'd said. "I'm sorry, that didn't come out right."

She laughed. "I knew what you meant. Scott, I'm not holding a grudge against you. I got over what happened between us a long time ago. That's water down the river."

His blue gaze bored into hers and he said softly, "I wish that wasn't true."

Hannah swallowed. Her words weren't completely honest but she didn't want him to know that. Truthfully, their night still hung between them, but now wasn't the time to get into it.

As they left their trays on the cleaning rack Hannah said, "Thank you for the meal. It hit the spot." She looked up at him. "Even with the questions."

"You're welcome. I'd like to make one more start toward earning your friendship by seeing that you get home safely. I'll get someone to take you home. You don't need to be driving, but I'm on call and can't leave."

"There's no need."

"You're worn out. You need to go home."

"I'm staying here."

Scott leaned forward. She could see the lines around his eyes, indicating he'd smiled a lot through the years. Probably at all the women he'd seduced. She'd do well to remember that.

"Hannah," he said earnestly, "you need to rest, which you won't do here. Wouldn't you like to sleep in your own bed? Pick up some clean clothes? Take a hot shower?"

He'd known what would get to her. A shower sounded heavenly.

After sighing deeply, she said, "I'll go. For tonight."

"I know you'd like to see Jake one more time before you leave. I'll call up and let Jake's nurse know you're coming. While you're gone I'll arrange your transportation and meet you in the lobby."

Hannah made her way through the maze of corridors back to CICU. At a set of automatic doors she spoke into the monitor on the wall and requested entrance into the unit. She'd never been more acutely aware of hospital rules. It was her son in there, and she had to ask permission to see him. As a nurse, she'd never realized how much control she'd had over a patient's life.

At Jake's bed, she whispered goodnight to her sleeping child and gave him a kiss.

Her baby...needed...a heart. If not...

She refused to let that thought catch hold.

Scott stood at one side of the lobby, talking on his phone, when Hannah approached a few minutes later. As if he sensed her arrival, he turned and looked at her. He ended the conversation and started forward.

Watching him saunter down the long corridor of the hospital used to be a favorite pastime of hers. She still found it absorbing.

As he approached, he smiled. "Your carriage is waiting."

Taking her elbow, he ushered her out the sliding glass doors at the front of the hospital. Waiting beside one of the hospital's vans was a security guard.

"Hannah, this is Oscar. He's going to be escorting you home."

The large, toothy man smiled. "Nice to meet you, Ms. Hannah. Climb in." Oscar opened the door nearest her then went around to the driver's side.

"I thought I was taking a taxi."

"Hush and appreciate the ride. Oscar believes he owes me a favor, so this is my way of letting him think he's paying me back."

"I'm grateful for the ride, but I don't understand why you're going to so much trouble."

"Let's just say I need to do it for me more than you. This way everyone wins." Scott helped her into the van. "You get a safe ride home with someone I trust, and Oscar gets to feel good about what he's doing. I'll see you tomorrow. I'll keep an eye on Jake and let you know if you're needed. Trust me."

Trust him? She'd trusted him one time with her affection and her body. He'd disappointed her. Could she trust him with Jake's life?

Oscar returned to her house early the next morning to bring her back to the hospital. He informed her that Dr. Mac expected it. Hannah agreed to the service, not wanting to hurt the sweet man's feelings.

At the hospital, she killed time in the waiting area until she could visit Jake. Her heart skipped when she saw Scott. She stepped toward him, pushing panic away, and asked, "Has something happened to Jake?"

His hand cupped her shoulder. "He's fine. I've spent most of the night in the unit, so I've been close by. He was sleeping when I left. You can go back to see him just as soon as shift change is over."

Hannah released an audible breath.

Scott held out a box of donuts. "I was hoping to find you. I thought you might like these. The 'Hot' sign was on."

"Did you go out especially to get these?"

"Yeah, but the bakery is just a few miles away. I promised the nurses I'd bring them some today. And I remember how crazy you were about them."

Hannah took the box. "You are really going above and beyond the call of duty on this being-a-friend thing." She looked up at him. "I really can use one right now. Ah, and they're still warm. Thanks for remembering." She brought the box up to her nose and inhaled deeply.

"I remember everything about you." He smiled, as a pensive look came over his face.

Heat rushed to her cheeks and she avoided his gaze. She didn't want to be sucked in by his charisma again, but he was making it awfully difficult not to be. "I thought you could use a blast of sugar to keep you going today. I've got a couple of minutes before I have to be in surgery. How about sharing those…" he nodded his head toward the box of donuts "…and a cup of coffee with me?"

"Sure, the parents' lounge has a coffee machine and a table and chairs. How about we go there?"

"Sounds great." He grinned.

It was still early enough in the day that they had the lounge to themselves. Scott's bulk filled the small area, making her conscious of how large a man he was, his scent reminding her of being outdoors after a rainstorm.

He sat at the small table after her. Hannah placed the box of donuts in front of him, and grinned as he struggled to work his long legs under the table. He gave up and stretched them out in front of him.

Sharing an intimate breakfast with Scott was

something she'd expected to do that morning after they'd made such passionate love. By a twist of fate, instead she was sharing a meal with him years later in a pitifully utilitarian room of a hospital with nothing more than tentative friendship between them. She forced the emerging hurt to one side.

She crossed to the automatic coffee machine and poured two cups of coffee.

"You don't have to pay?"

"No, this is here for the parents." She smiled. "Maybe they'd let you get a cup here the next time you're out of change and I'm not around."

A disquieted look came over his face for a second, and then he said, "That's a thought. I'm going to remember this place."

Placing their cups on the table along with some napkins, Hannah took a chair at the table. She really looked at Scott for the first time that morning. Absorbed his appearance. He looked incredible, even after a night with little sleep. He'd always been intriguing, larger than life, and that hadn't changed. If anything, he'd become more appealing.

Dressed in jeans that had seen better days and

a yellow snug-fitting T-shirt with "Come Paddle with Me" printed in bright red letters across his chest, Scott looked nothing like the white-coated doctor she knew him to be. His hair was a crowd of unruly waves, with a lock falling over his forehead.

Did he still spend his days off kayaking and rafting? He'd loved the water and adventure when he'd been in school. After rounds, he had sometimes come by the nurses' station and told her a funny story about something that had happened on one of his trips down the river. She'd always looked forward to those stories, because he'd shared them with such flair, making her wish she could go with him some time.

"You're not dressed like you're going to work. More like you're going to the river."

Somehow the thought that he might not be around for the rest of the day bothered her. What if Jake needed him?

His soft laugh filled the room. "These are my spare clothes. I keep them in a locker for nights like last night. Nothing was wrong with Jake."

Relief filled her. He wasn't going anywhere.

"You must be getting plenty of time in down

the river because you haven't changed much in the last eight years."

"Why, thank you for noticing." He dipped his head in acknowledgement. "I don't kayak as much as I'd like but that's where I usually spend my days off."

"I see your ego is still in good shape."

"It isn't as large as you might think," he said softly.

Had something happened that had damaged his confidence? "Was your night so difficult that you didn't go home?"

"Not bad, just constant."

From his causal demeanor, she would have never guessed he'd spent the night at the hospital.

"We got a new patient."

It made her chest tighten to think how the parents of the child must be feeling. Had it just been yesterday morning that she'd been in the same spot?

Scott opened the green and white box containing the donuts and pushed it toward her. "Ladies first."

Hannah picked out one sugary ring. She took a healthy bite and shoved the box toward him.

"You know what I've been doing for the last

few years—how about you?" He picked out a chocolate-covered one.

Hannah didn't want to talk about the last few years. The future was what she was interested in, one where Jake was better and at home. She'd tell Scott the bare facts to satisfy him, and hope he'd leave the subject alone.

"Well, since we worked together I received my MBA in nursing, got married, got pregnant, got divorced and moved to Atlanta after getting a job at Fulton Medical. And here I am." She raised her hands in the air in a dramatic pose.

That sounded like a well-rehearsed litany of events, even to her ears.

"Have you tried to contact his father since Jake was listed? I'd want to know if my son needed a transplant."

"No." The word came out jagged and tart.

"Why?"

Yes, why? Why wouldn't he leave it alone? "He wouldn't be interested." She couldn't conceal her bitterness.

"Why not?"

Hannah took her time finishing the bite of donut she'd just taken before she said, "He left us." She paused. "I shouldn't have married him to begin with. I think I just fell in love with the idea of being married. For him, I think his mother thought I could settle him down. By the time I realized we had no business being married, I was pregnant. Turns out I didn't have to leave him. He packed his bags and was gone. I found out later he already had someone else by then."

Scott's harsh, crude words filled the space between them.

"I couldn't agree with you more. He wasn't too sure about having children to begin with and when Jake was born with a heart problem he couldn't get past the idea that his child wasn't perfect. His answer was to run." She made it sound like she was giving a statement to a newspaper reporter. Just the facts. "Anyway, I have Jake, and he's the best thing that has ever happened to me. He's my life. All I've got. I won't lose him too."

"We'll do our best to get Jake out of here soon."

"I sure hope so." She picked out another donut. Her eyes closed in delight as she took the first bite out of it.

"Like these, do ya?" The words were filled with Scott's mirth.

She opened her eyes and nodded as she licked the sticky sweetness from her upper lip, and began to flick away the grains of sugar that had fallen on her chest.

Scott's laughter stopped as his eyes followed her movements.

An uncharacteristic warmth settled over her. The fine hairs at the nape of her neck stood as straight as corn on her granddaddy's farm. She tried to concentrate on what she was doing. Seconds ticked by.

His gaze rose and locked with hers, held.

Scott's pupils had widened and darkened, giving him the intent look of a predator. Suddenly, the light button-down top she wore seemed heavy and hot against her skin.

Mercy, she was in over her head. He could still do it to her. She placed her donut on a napkin and stood. "Um, I think I need some cream for my coffee. Can I get you some?"

She needed to move away from him, get out of the room, but she had to pass Scott to do so. His intense look still clung to her.

"It hurts you don't remember I take my coffee

black," he said in the indulgent voice of a man who knew she was trying to escape and why.

Hannah moved to step over his legs at the same time he drew them in. Her feet tangled with his. Falling, her head landed on his chest. The quaking of Scott's low rumble of amusement only added to her frustration, compounded by the molten heat she felt from being against him.

A zing of awareness zipped through her. It was happening again, just like it had all those years ago. Despite her embarrassment, Hannah longed to stay. She struggled not to show a response to the continued emotional assault, but she had to stop this now. If she didn't, it would end no differently than it had last time. With heartache— hers. Pushing against Scott's muscular thighs, she made an ineffectual effort to stand.

"Hannah, stop struggling and I'll help you up."

The words reverberated pleasantly beneath her ear. She stilled. He gripped her shoulders, pushing her away until she found her footing.

"Thanks," she murmured.

Scott stood, maintaining eye contact. "My pleasure. I rather like having you sprawled across me." As he closed the bottom button of his lab coat he said, "I'd better go check on a patient."

The nuance of his words and the heat of his touch lingered well after he'd disappeared down the hall.

CHAPTER THREE

WATCHING the clock, Hannah called to see if she could see Jake the second the minute hand clicked to eight. The clerk said she could come in, but she would have to stay at least thirty minutes because Scott was doing a procedure on a patient and couldn't be interrupted.

The automated doors swooshed opened when Hannah pushed the silver entry button on the wall. She went straight to Jake's cubicle. He was still asleep. Hannah placed a kiss on his forehead and the nurse told her that he'd had a good night.

She wanted to believe that a heart would be available soon. Scott had spoken with such confidence that one would be found. For her own sanity, she was desperate to trust him. Searching for something positive to cling to, Scott's optimism was all she had. Yet Hannah wasn't ready to believe him without question. If she lost Jake...

Dropping into the chair next to Jake's bed, she

looked out into the unit. From her vantage point, she had a direct view of Scott.

He'd changed into scrubs. Holding a mask in his latex-covered hand, he said to the nurse beside him, "Has she been given meds?"

"The morphine and Pavulon are on board," the young nurse responded.

Donning the mask with the nurse's help, Scott gave calm orders in a crisp tone that generated an instant response.

Hannah was impressed by the way he managed the situation, but not surprised. Scott demanded attention out of respect, without being dogmatic. Being witness to how he remained cool in a literal life-and-death situation reassured her. The staff followed his lead.

These attributes were priceless in the operating room. No wonder she'd heard such glowing reports about his abilities. A surgeon had to have the respect of the people who worked with him.

Scott raised the edge of the dressing covering the child's open chest. "Patch."

The nurse at his right handed him the six-by-six white bandage. He placed it over the incision.

Despite her lingering cynicism, Hannah appreciated Scott's efficient but tender manipulations as he worked with the infant child. She'd always admired the way he'd had a gentle touch for his patients and had gone to great lengths to make them feel comfortable.

Scott had done the same with Jake and herself. He'd been nothing but caring and helpful towards them both.

Over his shoulder, Scott spoke to the clerk behind the desk. "Call OR. Tell them we're coming down in fifteen." He turned back to the nurse. "Thanks for the help."

The nurse nodded and smiled.

Scott stepped away from the bed, pulled off the mask and gloves, then removed his gown with minimal effort, before tossing them into a basket. The actions were automatic. Hannah found the ordinary spellbinding when Scott was involved. It was like watching a thoroughbred horse go through his paces. She couldn't help but be riveted.

Going to the row of sinks on the wall, he scrubbed before moving to another patient's bed, where he spoke to a nurse. When he was finished, he approached Hannah.

She stood and asked in a hushed voice, "Is the baby going to be all right?" As irrational as the thought pattern was, when another child wasn't doing well, Hannah felt like it might rub off on Jake. As if heart problems were contagious.

"Yes, she should be fine with time. How's Jake doing?"

"Sleeping peacefully, but I think he may be breathing heavier."

"Let me have a listen."

Hannah watched as he examined Jake.

When Scott had finished he turned to her. "He may be having a little more difficulty. I'll have the nurse keep a closer eye on him."

Scott flipped the stethoscope around his neck and took her by the elbow, leading her away from Jake's bed to a corner of the room where they couldn't be easily seen.

His look sobered, telling her he was debating whether or not to say something.

"What's wrong? You're scaring me."

"I wasn't sure if I should tell you, but I had a call about a possible heart for Jake a few minutes ago."

Hannah grabbed his arm and squeezed. "You did?" It was the first time she'd voluntarily touched him. Scott just wished it had been for another reason.

He wanted to reassure her, make her understand. "Yes, but it wasn't good enough. I had to turn it down."

Disappointment, disbelief, and fear all showed in her eyes before anger pushed them away. Her fingers tightened on his arm, biting into his skin. "What? You can't do that." She glanced around as if she were caged and looking for a way out.

Scott hated having to telling her. He'd anticipated this reaction. Unable to wrap his arms around her, he took her hand. "It'll be fine." Softening his voice as if to calm a scared animal, he added, "I want the best heart we can get for Jake. The right one will come."

He believed that, but wanted her to accept it as truth. To have faith in him again.

She pulled her hand away, clasped her hands together and looked straight ahead. "I hope you're right."

The sharpness of her voice cut him.

"Hannah, I can't imagine how hard this must be." His fingers wrapped her forearm, unable to keep from touching her. "I'll take good care of Jake. I'll get him the right heart. Trust me."

"Dr. McIntyre," the clerk called.

Scott let his hand drop and stepped away from Hannah.

"Dr. Stevens would like to speak to you and the OR called to say they're ready," the clerk finished, giving them a speculative look.

Scott regretted the interruption. "Please tell Dr. Stevens I'll call him as soon as possible and let the OR know I'll be down in a few minutes." He shocked himself. He'd never said anything but, "I'll be right there."

Hannah needed him and neither of the other issues was an emergency.

"Hannah, please sit down." She eased into a chair, and he pulled a rolling stool up close.

He unclasped her hands, taking one and smoothing her fingers out across his palm. Lowering his voice, he said, "The perfect heart for Jake will come. You just have to believe that. He's stable for now. We have to wait on the right one."

"I know. I understand. I just don't like it."

He ran a finger along her jaw, making her look at him. "That's my Hannah, tough when you have to be. I hate to leave you but I have to go. I have a patient waiting in surgery."

"I know. I understand. That little baby needs you. I'll be fine."

Guilt gnawed at him for having to leave her when she needed him but he had no choice. When duty called he would always go.

Scott entered the large open area of the waiting room and stopped. The nurse had said the parents were here. He wished he could delegate this job to someone else, but that wasn't the way he worked, or would let himself work. Despite feeling inadequate, it was still his responsibility to talk to the mother and father of his little patient.

He'd let his mother down when she'd needed him, and he wouldn't do the same with the parents of any of his patients. Sometimes he wondered if his struggle to speak to the family was his penance for failing his mother so miserably. Was it his way of atoning for past mistakes, to involve himself so totally with his patients?

The surgery on the girl had been more difficult than anticipated but the medical whys and wherefores wouldn't mean anything to the girl's parents. They were only interested in him fixing the problem and making sure their daughter went home with them. It wasn't, unfortunately, that simple.

He understood their fears, sympathized with

them, sometimes to his own emotional detriment. Caring so profoundly made him a sought-after surgeon but it left nothing to give to others. He'd heard that complaint on more than one occasion from a woman.

Scott searched the area again. He scanned past a person, and came back. *Hannah.* He'd not seen her since earlier that morning.

His gaze met hers. She sat up ridged in her chair. *She thinks I've come to give her bad news.*

Summing his most reassuring smile, he watched as the tension drained from her like a rubber band being released. Her chest rose as she took a deep breath and let it out slowly. She met him halfway across the room.

"Jake's fine. I just checked on him. He was even sitting up and playing with his bear."

"Thank goodness." Hannah gave him a weak smile. "From the look on your face, something is wrong. Are you okay?"

"I should be asking you that."

"I'm all right. Just don't be turning down too many hearts."

"I won't, I promise."

"So what's putting that frown on your face?"

Her hand made contact with his forearm for a second.

The simple gesture calmed him, giving him confidence. Telling him it was all right to care. "How did you know?"

"I've always been able to tell when you were upset."

"Yeah, you were good at that. You were the one nurse who was willing to go with me when I talked to parents."

"Thankfully, that didn't happen too often."

Scott glanced around the room and found the couple he'd been looking for in the far corner. "I've got to speak to those parents."

As he turned to leave, Hannah touched his arm again. "You're better at talking to parents than you think. The truth is always hard to take, but they'll want to know it and will appreciate you giving them honesty."

"Thanks." Hannah's words were gratifying, making what was coming seem less daunting. She made him believe he was up to the task.

He'd always cared too much for his own good about his patients, unable to keep a professional distance like other physicians. It became more of an issue after his mother's overdose. The next morning in the hospital she'd made some ugly accusations about him. When she'd shouted that he'd abandoned her for his own patients, just like his father had, and she didn't need Scott any more either, he'd felt like he'd been slapped.

He'd seen that she received the care and services she needed and became absorbed in his work. Their relationship still wasn't what it should be. He wished for more but it was difficult to put the unpleasant words she'd thrown behind him completely. If he had a question about his ability to manage a high-pressure career and a solid relationship, after that morning he'd known beyond a shadow of a doubt he couldn't. Even his own mom wanted little to do with him after he had disappointed her.

But he refused to disappoint his little patients' families. Squaring his shoulders, Scott made an effort to look less like a man bearing bad news and walked toward the girl's parents. Hannah watched Scott approach the couple. They stood, but he waved them down before he sat. He raked his hand through his hair, leaving a wavy lock hanging across his forehead, adding to his vulnerable look.

Elbows on knees, Scott leaned forward, occasionally raising a hand to punctuate a point. He maintained eye contact with the mother and spoke in a low tone. One filled with compassion, she was sure. She'd heard the caring there when he'd told her Jake needed a heart.

He appeared confident, but she knew better. In the past, they'd talked a number of times about how difficult it was for him to speak with parents. She'd tried to reassure him, telling him that feeling so deeply for the patients and their families was part of who he was and what made him a good doctor.

The mother's shoulders jerked up and down and Scott reached out and touched her. She turned to her husband, and he took her in his arms.

Hannah's sympathy went out to the three. Scott looked like he was the one that needed a friend. She was tempted to go over and take Scott's hand, be his moral support.

She'd had a taste of his bedside manner when he'd held her. Based on what she'd learned about him during their reacquaintance, he wouldn't be a doctor who didn't tell it like it was, even if he had bad news. He'd always felt more deeply than he let on. They'd talked about different patients' problems in the past. Hannah had been able to tell by the tone of Scott's voice when he'd taken a patient's issues more to heart than he should have. Not being able to heal every person had worried him more than it had the other interns.

Scott was a soft touch with a hard outer covering, and was careful not to let that gooier side show. If he appeared weak, then the patient would feed off that. Their will to get better would be diminished and Scott wouldn't allow that. She'd often wondered if he was so cavalier in his personal life because he was trying to compensate for how deeply he cared for his patients.

He might have been, maybe still was—despite his implied remarks in the negative—a playboy but he'd always had a kind heart. She wasn't sure why he had treated her the way he had. Had she done something wrong to make him leave that morning? Only looking back on it, that really hadn't been like him.

Scott rose and spoke to the mother again. The woman nodded. Scott didn't even look in Hannah's direction as he left. He hurt for the parents, and that about Scott hadn't changed.

He'd comforted her yesterday. Today she wanted to run after him, reassure him. Maybe she'd been too hard on him? He'd been a great friend before and he seemed to be trying hard to be one again.

Who did Scott go to when he needed to talk through his problems?

Maybe she could at least make an effort to meet him halfway. She could use a friend right now, a shoulder to lean on. Could he also use one?

Hannah remained in the waiting room a while longer before going to visit Jake. It was quiet in CICU but she noticed two nurses and one of the interns standing beside the bed of a patient. It must be the child Scott was concerned about.

The parents had to be terrified.

She found her usual chair and settled in. Already she'd slipped into a hospital routine. The hours of waiting dragged by and the sky darkened as the sun set. The only thrill in the day was when she got to hold Jake for a short while. She craved the closeness of having him in her arms. Even now she missed his little body nestling next to hers.

Jake's nurse pulled Hannah out of her staring stupor with the statement, "I need to change Jake's IV. It's not flushing as it should."

Light-headed when she stood up, Hannah shook it off and moved to the bedside opposite the nurse. Hannah watched as the nurse removed the old IV port and began inserting a needle into a vein near Jake's wrist. Bright red blood dripped from the port onto the bed before the nurse could cap it off.

Hannah's stomach rolled like a wave hitting the shore. She'd witnessed IV ports being placed hundreds of times, done them herself more often than she could count, yet this was her son's blood.

Come on, Hannah. Keep it together.

She gripped the bedrail.

This is nuts. I'm an experienced nurse.

Closing her eyes, her head spun. Her body swayed. Opening her eyes wide, she focused on a spot on the white wall and took a gulp of air. Her grip on the rail became painful. The whirling worsened.

Her world went black.

Was that a hand pushing her hair off her forehead? There it was again. Opening her eyes a slit, Hannah could only make out a tiled ceiling. There was also a hard bed beneath her. Where was she? How had she gotten here?

Fainted. She'd fainted. She couldn't believe it.

A scraping noise of metal chair legs being moved across the floor caught her attention.

Turning her head towards the sound, she saw a pair of khaki-covered legs.

Her gaze lifted past sprawled legs, to the hem of a white pressed cotton lab coat with an unfastened bottom button. Her eyes followed the row of secured buttons to the open neck of a light blue shirt that looked familiar, over a square chin covered in enough evening shadow to be TV sexy, to full lips where a faint smile rested below a Roman nose and arresting eyes. They peered at her with a mixture of frank concern, humor, and maybe...longing.

Scott.

Could she be more embarrassed? Putting her hands over her face, she said between her fingers in a strangled voice, "Oh, no."

"Are you all right?"

"I'm fine. Just mortified." She groaned. "I've never fainted before in my life."

His soft chuckle would've made her knees go weak again if she'd been standing. He propped an elbow on a knee and put his chin in his hand, bringing his face closer. His eyes twinkled. "It's okay. Don't worry about it. We see it in the unit pretty often."

She shook her head in denial. "But I'm a nurse. It shouldn't be a problem for me!"

After a tap at the door, an aide entered with a soft drink can in one hand and a glass of ice in the other. Scott took both, setting them on a table.

"Is there anything else I can get or do?" She glanced at Hannah with concern.

"Thanks, Susie. No, I think Mrs. Quinn's going to be fine."

The aide left, closing the door behind her.

Hannah moved to sit up. Scott put a hand on her shoulder in gentle deterrence. The heat of his hand seeped through her cotton top like the sun on a hot day. That comforting warmth was becoming addictive.

"You need to stay put a few more minutes. We don't want you to fall and hurt yourself."

Resigned, Hannah settled back. "Where am I?"

"In the on-call attending's sleep room." Scott stretched back in the chair, extended his legs and folded his arms across his chest. He acted as if he was in no hurry to leave.

"How'd I get here?" Hannah murmured.

He gave her a cheeky grin. "I carried you."

"You did?" She hid her face. She hated the

thought of facing the people in CICU after that show.

"Yeah. I was coming through the doors when I saw your knees buckle. I managed to catch you before you hit the floor."

"Th-thanks," she stammered.

"I wish I could say I've always been as aware of people's needs, but I can't. I was just lucky to be in the right place at the right time."

"Whatever it was, I appreciate it. How's Jake?"

"He's just fine. Fared much better than you. He's a tough kid."

"I guess you think I'm a complete basket case after yesterday's show and now this today."

"Truthfully, I'm impressed with how well you're holding it together. I know of others with much less stress that haven't coped nearly as well as you."

The compliment brought a glow of pleasure. Had he been thinking about an old girlfriend, friend or family member?

"Let's see if you can sit up now." He reached out and helped by supporting her back as she righted herself, though Hannah wasn't sure the physical contact wasn't putting her further off center.

"I'm fine. You don't have to baby me, even if I seem like one." She moved away from his hand.

She didn't want to contemplate her strong reaction to Scott's touch. Heaven help her, having Scott's attention was getting to her. Maybe this thing she had about him was her mind's way of helping her remain sane. Giving her something to dwell on besides Jake.

Scott stood, pushing his chair out of the way. Pouring the soft drink into the cup, he offered it to her.

Hannah looked flushed, but beneath it a healthy color had returned. Was the pink from embarrassment or because he remained so close? Maybe both?

Setting the cup on the table, she tried to stand. She plopped back on the low bed.

The next time he slid his hand around her waist as she stood. "Let's try that again, a little slower." He left her no opportunity to move away from him. "Better? Head bothering you?"

Scott sucked in a breath as the gentle heat of her body pressed against him. The yearning to lean into her grew. Under his scrutiny, Hannah looked away but, using a finger under her chin, Scott brought her focus back to him. Her moss-colored eyes had darkened, and she blinked.

Heaven help him, he wanted to kiss her. Unable to stand the tug of need any longer, he leaned towards her.

Hannah's eyes widened as his mouth lowered to hers.

Fearing she might push him away, he placed his lips lightly at the corner of her mouth, tasting, testing, and asking for her acceptance.

A hot flare of desire flashed through him. History was repeating itself, and he was incapable of stopping it.

Scott wanted Hannah as much as he had that night so many years ago. His hands shook with the depth of it. She was a soft yet demanding siren, drawing him. Her vulnerable appearance masked an iron strength he admired. He'd fought his desire once but he couldn't do it twice. His emotions drove him, his mind was no longer in control. He had to savor her once more.

Her lips parted, and he gave thanks for the opportunity. He took the invitation offered and pulled her tight against him, bringing his lips down to completely capture hers.

Seconds ticked by before her hands ran along

his arms, stopping at his biceps, squeezing them slightly as if to steady herself.

She tasted of tea, lemon, and well-remembered Hannah. He felt a quake of emotion ripple through her as her fingers flexed on his arms. No longer able to hold himself in check, his desire flowed over its banks. Without constraints the kiss escalated into a crushing assault.

Hannah shivered, and Scott groaned low in his throat. This was going to get out of hand if he didn't put a stop to it. He didn't need to ruin the cautious friendship they were building again.

Hannah clung to him. Having her in his arms was a heady feeling.

He had to put a stop to the fever threatening to become wildfire out of control. Easing his mouth from hers, he tenderly brushed his lips across hers as he murmured, "What are you doing to me?"

He knew he'd missed their friendship but he'd not realized how much he'd missed touching her, having her in his arms. "I've thought a lot about kissing you since this morning," he muttered. "You make eating a donut look incredibly sexy." He glanced at the hard, narrow bed behind her. *The* question flickered in his gaze.

Hannah squirmed and he eased his hold. He watched the rapid throb of her pulse on her delicate neck.

If he asked the question out loud, would she?

Long, sizzling seconds hung between them. Scott closed his eyes then opened them again. Remorse washed over him. He'd promised friendship, she'd made her expectations clear. She was the mother of one of his patients. What he was suggesting was wrong on many levels.

Scott stepped back, releasing her. "I'm sorry. I shouldn't have done that. You had my word we'd remain just friends. I think we're both experiencing emotional overload." The words came out flat and measured. "Please, forgive me."

She smiled shakily. "You're forgiven. I think it's the least I can do for someone who brings me hot donuts."

Hannah was on her way through CICU to visit Jake for the last time that evening. She'd relived the kiss between her and Scott numerous times. She understood he was just being human, that maybe he'd needed someone after the day he'd had. As a way to let off steam. But somehow his apology for kissing her felt worse than being left in bed alone.

She couldn't be mad at him. He'd been so wonderful with Jake and had cared for her when she'd needed a shoulder to cry on. That tenderhearted person she'd known before had still been in him when he'd spoken to those parents.

As she reached Jake's cubicle a deep baritone growl filled the air. The sound was followed immediately by a roll of giggles she recognized. *What was going on?*

She stopped short at the sight of Scott sitting in a rocker with Jake in his lap. Scott held a book so Jake could see the pictures. Neither of them noticed her as she stood in the doorway.

"And the pig goes…"

"Oink, oink, oink," Jake said with a big smile. "You do."

"And the bear goes grrrr…" Scott drew the sound out.

Hannah had never expected to find Scott taking the time to read to any of his patients. She enjoyed listening to his rough voice as he read to Jake. The sight and sounds of the two of them having a good time together soothed nerves that had been piano-wire-taut.

"And the horse goes?"

"Me do, me do. Heehaw, heehaw."

Scott's deep chuckle made her feel mushy inside. He was enjoying himself as much as Jake was. Her heart softened. She ran a finger under her eye. Once again Scott had managed to push the unpleasantness of what was happening to Jake away for just a few minutes. Her son was a kid, instead of just a patient.

"More. Me do," Jake said as he helped Scott turn the page.

"Okay, how does the chicken go?" Scott said as he smiled down at Jake.

"Cluck, cluck, cluck."

"Yes, that's right. Cluck, cluck, cluck. Smart boy."

Jake clapped his hands.

Scott looked up. Hannah couldn't help but grin at his disconcerted look. He shrugged his shoulders and grinned.

She smiled back, hoping to convey her appreciation. "Hi, guys. You two sound like you've been having fun."

"Mommy." Jake lifted his arms toward her.

"Hi, sweetheart." She stepped over to take him from Scott, being careful not to get tangled up in the IV lines. She pulled the little boy close for a hug. Jake was warm from being held by Scott.

"So, have you been having a good time with Dr. Mac?" she asked against his cheek before kissing him.

Jake nodded up and down. "He funny."

She looked at Scott and grinned. "He is, is he?"

Jake bobbed his head with enthusiasm.

"I was here when the Child Life lady came by with the books and the next thing I know I'm making animals noises."

She nibbled at her boy's neck. "Jake loves to have someone read to him."

Jake yawned.

"I think you might have had too much fun," Hannah said as she moved to Jake's bed and laid him down. His eyes were already closing as she kissed him on the cheek. He had such a small energy reserve. Despite the earlier lift to her spirits they were suddenly dampened by the reminder of why he was here.

Scott came to stand beside her. "He's a wonderful kid. You've done a great job with him, Hannah."

"Thanks. I think he's pretty outstanding too." She pulled the blanket up around Jake.

She looked away from him a few seconds later when she thought she'd heard Scott say Jake's mother was pretty amazing also, but he was gone.

Scott didn't want to tell her, but he had to. Hated what he had to say. Hated to see the little boy who had such a cute personality so sick.

Some patients he connected with better than others but Jake had captured his heart. Scott wanted to say it was because he was Hannah's son but that wasn't all there was to it. Jake's willingness to be held by him, to giggle when he was around, made Scott feel taller and stronger for some reason. It made his heart swell to see the boy grin up at him.

Hannah should be waiting on him in one of the consultation rooms down the hall. He'd had the clerk call her soon after she'd left the unit, asking her to wait for him. She had to be scared to death, wondering what was wrong. He lengthened his strides.

She was pacing the room when he opened the door.

"What's wrong? Can I see Jake?"

"He's okay but—"

"But what?" Fear sharpened her voice.

"I've given orders for Jake to be put on the respirator." He stepped closer to her. "Things are under control. He just needs a little help breathing."

She took a couple of halting breaths, and let out a soft moan.

"Hannah, honey, this is just a precaution. Jake's all right." His chest clenched at seeing her upset. He'd give anything to take the burden away.

She looked up. Even in the dim light he could see the moisture glistening in her big, sad eyes.

"W-w-will he be okay?"

Hannah was struggling bravely to keep her composure. Scott took her in his arms, pulling her securely against him. A tremor went through her, and a sob escaped. He couldn't really know her fear. He wasn't Jake's father. But he could comfort her, let her know she wasn't alone. When he placed a kiss on her temple, she made a soft, incoherent sound.

"We've got everything under control," Scott whispered as he took a handful of silky hair and moved it out of her face. "The fellow is a good man. He'll take care of Jake tonight." He tipped her chin up, drawing her focus. "This is nothing more than a precaution. Jake's breathing became labored and we don't want him to wear himself out before surgery. Hannah—" his tone gained her complete attention again "—a heart will come."

"I don't know how much more of this he can take. Or I can take," she murmured.

Scott skimmed a tear from her cheek with the pad of his thumb. "You're strong. You'll get through this. Trust me, we're doing all that can be done."

She leaned into him as if she was drawing strength from him.

Scott liked having her next to him for any reason. He tightened his embrace, needing the contact almost as much as she did. He lowered his voice to soothe and comfort. "We have everything under control." He sure hoped he was telling her the truth. All that could be done was being done, but sometimes things went wrong. He ran a hand across her shoulders and down her back. "You can—*we* can—get through this together."

He desperately needed her to feed off his confidence. To believe in what he said, in him. He wanted to be her haven, someone she turned to. Hannah nuzzled her cheek against his chest.

Dampness touched his skin. "I hope you're right." She shuddered against him, as if she was accepting that with him was where she should be.

Holding her close, he continued to whisper nonsense. Despite all his skill as a surgeon, there were times he still felt helpless. He wished he could prevent what Jake was going through, but that was out of his power. Hannah needed support, and he would see that she got it.

He wasn't going to make the same mistake twice with someone he cared about. He'd misread how emotionally depressed his mother had been, and he refused to take the chance of doing the same with Hannah. The first time there had been major repercussions to his inaction. He would not repeat it. He couldn't promise that he'd be there for her for ever, but the least he could do was to be here for her now.

This time he would make time. At this moment he had no doubt he was needed, and he refused not to act on it. Regret was something he wasn't prepared to live with. But there was a major difference between the two women. His mother had demanded his attention and Hannah was pushing him away.

He breathed a sigh of relief when she moved.

She turned her back to him, took a deep breath and squared her shoulders. "I'm okay now." He couldn't help but admire her. She was already gathering courage, preparing to fight her fears bravely again.

"Hannah," he said softly, "I know you're going to hate this suggestion, but I think you need to stay at my place tonight."

She spun to face him. "What? I can't do that!" The words had a ring of panic to them.

"Calm down. Hear me out. It's late and you're upset. Tired."

"I don't plan to go home. I bought a bag with me this morning. I'm staying at the hospital."

"No, you're not. You need a good night's rest. You'll stay at the hospital a lot after Jake's transplant. Anyway, my place isn't far away. You can be here in no time if you're needed. You can use my extra room."

A yawn escaped her, confirming visibly how drained she was. She covered her mouth. "I'm staying here."

"I don't think so." The words were said in a firm, blunt tone. His voice softened with the next ones. "Be reasonable Hannah. If you stay at my place you can visit a few minutes before shift change tomorrow morning."

"That's blackmail."

"Yes, it is. Now, come on."

CHAPTER FOUR

SCOTT'S condo was in a nice upscale area, but nothing over the top. Done out in beiges, tan and a touch of black, it had a masculine appearance, with the only hint of a woman's touch being two bright orange pillows on the sofa. What girlfriend had been responsible for those?

Outdoors magazines were strewn across the dark wood coffee table and the black leather sofa, and a shirt hung over a chair next to the door. The room had all the markings of bachelor living, of a person who didn't have time to waste on the small stuff in life.

She liked the place. It suited Scott.

"How about something to drink before we call it a night?" he asked as he threw his jacket on a chair and dropped her small overnight bag on the floor.

"A glass of iced tea would be nice, if you have it."

"Sure."

Scott led her to a kitchen lined with windows. It would be a perfect place to enjoy a leisurely breakfast but he probably never had time to do so. He pulled a pitcher of tea from the refrigerator and opened a cabinet. He was taking out two glasses when his cellphone rang.

"Hey, hold on a sec," he said into the phone, and then told Hannah, "I need to get this. Help yourself. I'll be right back."

"The hospital?"

"No, honey. It's one of my kayaking buddies. I'll be right back."

She had to stop overreacting every time Scott's phone rang. Relieved but with her nerves still unsteady, she began filling a glass with ice from the fridge door. As she placed the glass on the counter, it toppled and began rolling over the edge, leaving ice in its wake. She bent and fumbled with the glass, taken aback when an arm brushed her breast. A quiver like that of a bow with the arrow just released went through her. Scott clasped the glass before it shattered on the floor. Reaching around her, he put the glass back on the counter.

His body heat blanketed her from head to foot. Her body came to full attention.

She strengthened and looked at him. Their gazes met and held.

Scott's hands came to rest on her waist. Why she didn't argue, she couldn't fathom. Maybe because her mind was fuzzy, so completely filled with him. Or because she didn't want to.

He nudged her backwards, until her bottom pressed against the cabinet. Caging her in with an arm on each side, he trapped her between the hard surface of the cabinet and the equally firm plane of his body.

She should be pushing him away, but it felt good to be sharing someone's warmth. Being in Scott's arms calmed her nerves, pushed the worry away for a while.

His hands cupped her face. The slight tremor to his fingers made her understand the effort he applied to control his need. The pad of his thumbs caressed her cheeks. In a low and raspy voice he said, "I know I promised...but I can't quit thinking about this—you." He gathered her into a firm embrace before his mouth claimed hers.

Hannah made a soft sound of acceptance, and wrapped her arms around his waist. Her eyelids fluttered closed as her fingers kneaded his back. She leaned into the warm, sweet taste of his lips.

The memory of how he'd made her feel years ago and the sensation of his lips on hers earlier mingled together and made this kiss even sweeter.

The pressure of his mouth intensified, taking on a sense of urgency. Excitement filled her at the thought she made Scott spin out of control. He held her so tightly it was almost painful. The demand of his lips against hers was hard and unrelenting as he thrust his tongue into her mouth. A flurry and churn like that of a rocket going off swelled within her. Caught in the spinning sensations, she met his powerful demands with those of her own, and hung on for the marvelous ride. A pleasure-filled way to escape.

After the initial combustion of their lips meeting, Scott eased the kiss into a tender caress. Soothing, sinful and sensual all at once but Hannah missed the throbbing pressure and heat. She wanted more. To replace the debilitating fear and heartache, even if only for a few minutes.

Bringing her hands to his head and spreading her fingers to run through his hair, she guided his mouth closer, opening her own. Scott took and countered with a challenge of his own. He shifted closer, making the evidence of his longing clear.

A steady hum of pleasure built upon itself until it became an unrelenting, pulsating yearning. Unaware of anything else in her world, Hannah's only reality became what Scott's lips were doing to her.

She made small purring sounds.

Scott lifted her to sit on the counter. There was a clank as the glasses tumbled along the counter behind her.

He lifted his mouth. Resting his forehead against hers for a moment, he took a deep breath and let it out. He looked as regretful as she that they'd been interrupted.

Scott's gaze met hers. His eyes had turned a dark, velvety blue. "I think I'll pass on the iced tea and go for you." Still in a Scott-induced haze, Hannah fought hard to comprehend what he'd said. He'd twisted her thoughts around like a tornado going.

Hannah shook her head and looked away. Heaven help her, she was no more immune to his charm and desire than she had been as a young nurse. She had to clear her mind. "I think I'd better get down."

His mouth dipped towards hers. She stopped the motion with a hand on his shoulder. He didn't immediately back away but soon helped her down. She wobbled as she moved, then swayed. Scott released a low chuckle. Putting out a hand, he steadied her and with the other hand he swiped the ice cubes into the sink.

"As much as my ego would appreciate believing you're weak in the knees from my kisses only, I'm afraid some of it's because you're worn out. Come on. I'll show you where you can sleep." He kept a hand on her elbow as they moved down the hallway.

He stopped, opened a door wide and turned on the light.

"I'll go get your bag. That door over there is the bathroom. Make yourself at home. You should find everything you need in there." His arm brushed her as he pointed. "My mother usually keeps extra here for when she visits."

Hannah's breath caught. She balled her fingers to keep from reaching out and touching him. If she couldn't control her growing attraction, she'd embarrass them both. They needed to be comfortable around each other, for Jake's sake.

Just friends. That's what they were. If she repeated it enough maybe she would believe it. Despite the red-hot kiss.

Before she could do something she'd regret, he'd turned and headed toward the living room. She wanted to call him back. Beg him to kiss her again. Instead, she watched as his loose-hipped strides took him away.

Hannah sucked in a breath. *This has to stop.*

Scott looked confident and relaxed, while her insides quivered. She must've developed brain rot to have agreed to come to his place. He was too much. Heck, he made her feel too much.

Hannah stepped into the bedroom. It had the basics—bed, end table, and dresser. The navy spread and curtains were the out-of-a-package kind that could be found in any large household chain store. The room had the look of a functional but otherwise forgotten space.

Scott returned and handed her the bag.

"If you'll toss the clothes you have on into the hall, I'll throw them in the wash."

"Scott, I've needed a friend and you've gone out of your way to be a good one. I appreciate it."

He nodded. "You're welcome."

The husky thickness of his voice beckoned her. She wanted to step into his arms. Feel safe. The heat of their earlier kiss hovered, waiting to flare up again, like a spark starving for fuel.

He made no move to leave. "Hannah?"

As if he willed it, her gaze lifted to meet his.

"I'm sorry I treated you so badly back then, that you had such a lousy marriage, and that this is happening to Jake."

Hannah nodded, unable to say anything as he closed the door quietly behind him.

Going to the bed, she lay on it and covered her eyes with an arm. Her thoughts bounced around like ping-pong balls inside a lottery machine. She was caught up in the vortex called life. Jake needed a heart and Scott's mind-numbing kisses were becoming additive. The emotional pressure of having a child waiting on a heart transplant and this, this…

She couldn't even put a name to it. A crush? An attraction? Sexual desire? Why did these emotions have to be swelling all at the same time? It would be hard enough one after another. Her feelings were all tangled. Scott and Jake. Jake and Scott.

Scott cracked the door open, allowing a dim shaft of light into Hannah's room. Had he heard her call out?

"No, no, no," she cried as she tossed, kicking at the covers.

She was having a nightmare. He hurried to her. Sitting on the edge of the bed, he gathered her into his arms. She trembled. The musky, warm smell of sleep surrounded her.

The T-shirt she wore left an exposed expanse of slim thighs. Scott stared, feeling the first stirring of arousal. He couldn't have stopped looking for the world. His eyes remained riveted to where the edge of the T-shirt barely covered her panties. He summoned the presence of mind to say in an even tone, "Hannah, wake up. You're having a nightmare."

She opened her eyes but he could see she wasn't completely focused on him. "Scared."

"I know, honey. But I'm here now."

"Stay," came out in a pleading whisper.

His heart jerked to a stop before it found its pace again.

"Hold me."

Her quiet, pleading words tore at Scott's heart. He could help this time and he wouldn't let her down. He was being a friend. But they couldn't remain friends if she continued to snuggle up against him like he was her savior. It was difficult to keep her at arm's length physically as well as emotionally. His wasn't that strong. Taking a deep breath, he vowed to comfort her—nothing more.

Scott scooped her into his arms and placed her in the middle of the bed before crawling under the covers and snuggling her to him, her back against his chest. He'd never spooned with a woman before. Never stayed long enough to form a bond. Women had asked him to stay but he had always refused. His affairs had been more about physical release. Because he'd guarded his emotions so closely and refused to open up, all his relationships had slowly dissolved over time.

Hannah had already broken through one of the barriers he'd erected to distance women. He'd never experienced this kind of confusion before where a woman was concerned.

It felt good to have Hannah cloistered under the sheets alongside him as if he were fighting off her fiery dragons. She wriggled closer, then sighed deeply. Seconds later her breathing became soft and regular. He couldn't give in to his growing desire, refused to make promises he couldn't ever keep.

What would be next? Would she expect more

from him? Would he be disappointed if she didn't? He wouldn't like it if she was the one pushing him away.

He'd seen the damage a job like his did to a relationship. Others managed, but it wasn't in his genes to handle it. The chance he might fail Hannah and Jake was one he wouldn't allow himself. He couldn't have two people depending on him emotionally, just medically. He refused to let the demands of his career ruin their lives, because he couldn't reset his priorities.

Still…wouldn't it be heaven to have Hannah to come home to after a long night of emergency surgery?

Pain and pleasure warred within him. There would be no more sleep for him tonight.

Hannah woke with a start. She needed to check on Jake!

Snugly tucked against warmth, she wished she didn't have to move, but she had to find her phone. Riding quickly behind that thought was the realization that Scott's arms surrounded her. The solidness of his chest resting against her cheek was a sweet contrast to the gentle hand stroking her arm. Hannah felt a tender, dewy touch at her hairline. He'd kissed her.

She'd fallen asleep in Scott's arms! Even asked him to stay with her. In her bed. There were no social guidelines for what to do when you've begged a man to join you in bed. She had to maintain her self-respect, but checking on Jake took priority.

"Hannah?" Scott asked. The warmth of his voice swept across her cheek.

"I need to call the hospital."

The mattress shifted as he rolled away and back again. He handed her the cell phone she'd left on the bedside table. "I've already checked on Jake, but I know you want to hear for yourself."

Hannah punched the speed-dial number for the hospital. The phone rang.

Her heart beat in double time. Scott's arms no longer encompassed her, but he remained close enough that she could still feel his heat. She almost broke into hysterical laugher. How many mothers of transplant patients slept with the surgeon?

The nurse assured Hannah Jake was doing fine.

Had the nurse noticed how fast and shallow she was breathing?

Hannah disconnected the call, keeping her back to him.

"Are you all right?" Scott asked. "Jake is fine?" She could tell he'd moved out of touching distance.

"Yeah."

"Look at me," he said, sternly enough that she complied.

She tugged on the sheet as she sat up. Scott stood before her in a pair of red plaid boxer shorts. Her gaze moved past his bare chest, which she ached to run her hands across, and lifted until it met his eyes.

"You needed someone to lean on last night. You've nothing to be embarrassed about. So don't act as if you do."

She said nothing, her gaze locked with his. She licked her suddenly parched lips.

"Hannah..." Scott stepped toward her, passion flaring in his eyes. He halted beside the bed and looked down at her. The question hung in the air.

Time stood still between them.

She'd been forced by circumstances to trust Scott with her son's care, but had he changed enough that she could trust him where her heart was concerned? Could she take that chance again?

When she said nothing he took a deep resigned breath and said, "Why don't you get dressed? We still have time to get to the hospital before shift change. We can check on Jake together."

CHAPTER FIVE

SCOTT stepped into the bedroom, carrying Hannah's freshly laundered clothes as he'd promised. The hairdryer was buzzing in the bathroom so she was still in there. He laid the clothes on the bed. What would her reaction be if she stepped out and found him there?

Those precious, heartbeat-suspending seconds when he'd stepped toward the bed slipped into his thoughts. A tingle of anticipation still lingered. He'd wanted to return to her warmth, had all but begged to. Had she had to force herself to say no? From the look in her eyes, he thought she might have. What had kept her from saying yes? Did she still not trust him? If he had been in her shoes, he probably wouldn't either.

Was she still embarrassed about last night? To have her begging him to join her, to hold her had been so out of character for her. He was glad he'd been the one here when she'd needed someone.

She was no weak ninny who pleaded for comfort often. If she was out of control enough to ask him to stay then she was really hurting. This morning she had to be working to regain her pride.

He'd tried to put her at ease in the kitchen, which was next to impossible since he was humming with need like a taut wire in the wind. He'd held her because she'd needed it, despite it being unbearably difficult for him to stop there. She'd needed companionship and caring, not a lusty male. He'd been the gentleman last night that he should have been years ago. At least he'd made sure he'd still been there when she'd woken up this time.

His eyes lingered on the bed a second before he walked out the bedroom door.

Five minutes later Hannah entered his living room. Dressed in jeans and a red T-shirt with a sweater draped around her shoulders, she looked like a fresh-faced sorority girl out for an afternoon of shopping. She carried her bag in her hand. He'd not seen her look lovelier.

With a gruff "Let's go," he took the bag from her and opened the front door. She gave him a quizzical look but said nothing. If he just didn't touch her again he could make it without turning around and pulling her back into the bedroom.

As they approached his car, Hannah said, "I see you got that BMW you were always talking about. You've definitely moved up in the world."

"Just a little."

She gave a little huff of disbelief. "From that worn-out car you used to drive to this beauty is more than a little."

Warm pleasure at her appreciation filled him, and he smiled. "I bought it after I finished my surgical training. The old car had given its all, so I had to let go."

"That happens with people too."

Scott studied her a moment. Was she thinking about how badly he'd treated her after she'd given him her virginity?

He didn't want to believe that. Guilt had become something that he lived with every day, but he wanted to believe that Hannah really had forgiven him.

Opening the passenger door, he let her scoot in before closing it, then put the bag in the backseat. He climbed in behind the wheel. Hannah had already buckled up and was running her hands across the leather seat.

He smiled. At least she liked his car.

The sky was just turning pink on the eastern horizon as Scott drove to the hospital. He and Hannah spoke little on the way. Scott let her out at the front door, saying he would meet her outside the unit.

"Okay. Uh...thanks for your—uh—help...last night."

"No problem." Scott waited for her to close the door before he drove away. He hated having to leave her there. Didn't like the feeling they were sneaking around. After all, nothing was going on.

Yeah, right. He had to be fooling himself. If she'd said the word they would be in bed together right now.

Scott watched as Hannah came down the corridor from where he stood waiting for her. "I've cleared it for you to stay for just a few minutes."

They walked together to Jake's bed. A machine making a puffing sound with a long tube leading to Jake's mouth was the new fixture beside his bed.

"I hate this machine."

"I know, but you also understand it is necessity."

Jake's small chest rose with a huff of the pump.

His eyes were opened but were glassed over from the drugs Scott had ordered to keep him calm. His small fingers flexed as he strained against the Velcro strips that secured his hands to the bed, preventing him from trying to pull out the tube. He struggled to speak and looked frustrated when he couldn't.

Hannah put her index finger in his palm. She trailed the back of her finger down his pale cheek. "Shh...honey, Mommy's right here. I love you." She repeated the words almost as a chant.

Jake fell asleep as they stood watching him. Seconds ticked by. Hannah glanced over her shoulder at Scott.

"You really are a wonderful mother. Jake's a lucky little guy to have you," Scott said softly.

"I'm just doing what any mother would do."

Scott knew better than that. "No, you're not. You're here, letting him know you love him, no matter what, and that's the important thing. You're always thinking of him and not just yourself."

"Doesn't every mother?"

"No." The word came out harsher than he'd intended. "Some mothers reject their children

because they aren't what they want them to be."
His mother certainly had.

She gave him a thoughtful look, then said, "I
can't imagine ever doing that to someone I love."

"I don't imagine you could." Hannah loved too
freely and unconditionally for it to be any other
way.

"I don't feel like a very good mother right now.
I can't do anything to help Jake."

"You will soon. A new heart will come." Scott
picked up the chart on the end of the bed and
looked at it. "He's just getting a little help. We
don't want him to wear himself out. He's on half
a liter of oxygen and five breaths."

"You do know Jake's more than what you read
on that darned chart."

"Yes, I'm aware of that." A tone of sadness entered his voice. "I hate to see him this way too."

"I'm sorry. I shouldn't have said that. I know
none of this is your fault. It's just nerves talking."
She looked at Jake.

"I won't hold it against you."

She gave Scott a wry smile, and he tried to return a reassuring one.

Her smile grew and reached her eyes. "Thanks,

I appreciate that. No more falling apart for me. I'm going to be a big girl."

"I think you're doing just great." He raised his eyebrows in a wolfish manner. "I don't mind helping out at all."

Hannah looked away, but he didn't miss her pink cheeks. "Hey, there's a hospital event being held downtown tonight to raise money for a new cardiac MRI. I have to attend. I was wondering if you might like to go with me?" Scott tried to insert a casual friendly tone to cover his eagerness to spend an evening with her.

"I don't think that would be a good idea."

He wasn't going to give up easily. "I'd have more fun if I were with someone, especially if that person was you." What he didn't say was that he only wanted to go with her. "You can't stay with Jake at night anyway. Come, please. Food and dancing. No pressure, you've my word." He put his hand up as if he were taking a pledge in court.

"I don't have anything to wear."

Scott's mouth lifted at the corners. "Searching for an excuse, are you? All you need's a nice dress. These events are usually fun and it'll take your mind off Jake for a couple of hours."

She shook her head. "I don't—"

"Look, we'll go late. At nine. After you have to leave CICU. It's not good for your health to be sitting and stewing twenty-four seven. Look what happened yesterday. I'm alone. You're alone. So why can't we do something together? For old times' sake?"

"I don't know…"

"A heart won't come any faster because you're sitting here day and night. I'll be paged if anything happens."

"Scott, you and I shouldn't be going out. I don't need any more emotional upheaval in my life." She laid her hands on the rail of Jake's bed.

His heart flip-flopped. "So I cause you emotional upheaval?" He lowered his voice. "Come on, Hannah. Just because you're taking a break from here doesn't mean you care any less about Jake."

She wrinkled her nose and pursed her lips. He grinned. That dig had hit home.

"I think our relationship should only have to do with Jake and the present."

Scott said nothing for a few of seconds, letting the space and time between them grow. "But it's not, is it? I don't normally have mothers of patients to my home. This thing between us is too powerful to ignore."

Hannah blinked, and blinked again. She was aware of the *thing* he was talking about.

He stepped closer. "You don't want me to have to go alone, now, do you?" He purposely sounded like a little boy pleading for his first puppy. "You've got some pretty intense days ahead. Why not have one night of fun while Jake's in good hands? It might help keep you sane." Scott shifted from one foot to the other. Was she going to turn him down? He'd never been more anxious to hear a yes to a date invitation.

"Okay, but only this one time."

He grinned in triumph, tempted to give the air a high five. "Gee, that's not the most enthusiastic response I've ever received but I'll take it. I'll have Oscar take you home. He'll be waiting out front. I'll see you at eight?"

"I thought you said nine."

"I did, but you don't need to be here after shift change anyway."

"It's nine or not at all. I want to stay until Jake goes to sleep."

"Okay, I'll accept that if you will make an effort to at least try to enjoy yourself this evening."

"All I can promise is that I'll do my best."

She gave him a slight smile. Genuinely relieved to hear a positive answer, he decided to leave well enough alone. He wasn't used to feeling insecure when asking someone out on a date.

The clerk and tech gave him a curious look as he left. Had they noticed his special interest in Hannah?

The single desk lamp provided the only illumination in Scott's windowless office. Resting his elbows on the desk, he covered his face with his hands. What was happening to him?

He'd promised Hannah they would keep it simple and easy. He shouldn't push for more. They had no future. He'd known all those years ago that she was the type of woman who would want to settle down and have a family. She would expect and deserved someone that could be there full time. Not someone with divided loyalties.

What would happen when he could no longer step away? She and Jake were slipping under his defenses. That didn't matter. He still had to let them go.

Heck, he'd not only fallen for the mother but her kid. Jake had managed to wrap him around his finger as well. Scott felt like a car being pushed by another one. No matter how hard he applied the brakes, he was still moving forward. He was in deep with no hope of getting out gracefully. Was it possible for him to have a solid relationship and still be the kind of doctor he wanted to be?

Hopefully if he got the position in Dallas, that would solve the problem.

He didn't want Hannah to be hurt again. When she'd made that comment about being let go he wasn't sure she'd been referring to years ago. Her ex had hurt her too. No wonder she was so cautious.

Scott understood why Hannah had been angry and distrustful of him initially, but she acted as if she was coming around. He'd been honored she'd trusted him enough to ask for help during the night.

It would've been fabulous to be inside Hannah's warm, welcoming body. Instead, he'd been left with a hunger that might drive him mad. A cold shower had been his reward for being a gentleman.

He'd not stayed around long enough the last time they'd been in bed together to enjoy the ruffled morning look that was so cute on Hannah. Now he wished more than ever he'd crawled back into her bed the morning after they'd made love.

Kissed and bedded the mother of a patient. It wouldn't have been a quick consoling trip down memory lane. He hardened at the memory of the vulnerability and longing that had been in her eyes. Once he'd started kissing that generous pink mouth, he wouldn't have stopped until they had both been satisfied. He'd have missed rounds for sure. And he never missed rounds.

Despite the gnawing longing, he refused to take advantage of her need for simple human contact. She was alone, in a stressful and fearful situation. She'd only been in his home because of her son. He wanted Hannah to desire *him*, not just let him into her bed because she needed someone.

Tapping on the open door drew his attention. Andrea entered. "Daydreaming, boss?" she asked with a grin.

If the truth be known she was more his boss than the other way around. As his right-hand woman, she kept him on track.

"Just thinking. Did you let UNOS know that Jake Quinn had been placed on the respirator?"

"I called just a few minutes ago."

"Good. I was...wondering if you would do me a favor."

"What's that?"

"Would you sit with Mrs. Quinn while the transplant is taking place? She has no one and I think she should have someone with her while Jake's in surgery. I need to know she is taken care of."

The protective part of him had been more pronounced since Hannah had re-entered his life. When he'd seen those sad, sorrow-filled eyes he'd wanted to take all her cares away.

"Sure, boss. I'll be glad to. This one's getting to you, isn't it?"

"Yeah, this transplant needs to go smoothly."

The one way he could achieve that goal was to make sure that Jake got better, and soon. He had no control over the allocation system, or the number of children on the waiting list, but he had control over the type of care Jake received. Confident in his abilities as a surgeon, he'd been right when he'd told Hannah not to worry. The odds were in Jake's favor.

"I wasn't referring to the patient."

Scott didn't respond. Andrea gave him a knowing smile and left him alone with his thoughts.

He needed to face facts—his greatest fear wasn't for Jake, but for his own heart when he had to give Hannah up. And he would give her up because he did care so much for her.

Scott groaned. He couldn't go around half-aroused all day. He leaned back in the chair and raked his fingers through his hair. The sexual tension between Hannah and himself was like no other he'd ever known. What he didn't understand was how she'd managed to flip his ordered and planned world upside down in a matter of days.

The doorbell dinged again.

"I'm coming," Hannah yelled, managing to make it into the living room just after the third ring. Swinging her front door wide, Hannah stood stunned by the sight of Scott, dressed in a navy suit.

Gorgeous. Breathtakingly handsome. All healthy male.

Scott looked like the cover guy on a magazine. The color of the suit deepened the blue of his eyes. The ones twinkling at her now.

His broad shoulders filled the entrance. She swallowed a "Wow," trying not to embarrass herself. A crisp white button-down shirt and a silk tie in striped shades of blues finished his impeccable appearance. He'd shaved that evening. She caught a hint of his earthy aftershave. She liked it.

What would he do if she ran her palm across the plane of his cheek? She shoved her hands into the pockets of her robe.

Scott's hair had been trimmed, but the thick waves were mussed. She grinned. He'd been running his fingers through it. He did that when he was anxious. Had he thought she wouldn't let him in?

He represented sophistication right down to the bouquet of yellow roses in his hand. Her favorite color. Right now Scott appealed to her more than a chocolate sundae on a hot Saturday afternoon. She could almost taste him.

"That good, huh?" A grin lined his full lips and broadened to a smile.

Hannah bit the inside of her cheek to keep "Yum" from seeping through her lips. "Good-looking suit."

"Just the suit?"

She waved her hand at him as if dismissing the question. "Stop fishing for compliments."

Scott's smile and laughter were a lethal combination, hard to resist. He was pulling her under his spell again, making her revisit all those feelings she'd long hidden, making her think, *What if?* Making her remember why they had been such good friends at one time. Why she'd enjoyed his company so much. Hannah hoped he had no idea of the magnitude of her mental and physical reaction to him.

She didn't want to feel anything for him. She'd already been there and done that, and had the broken heart to show for it.

"Come in. I'm not quite ready. I still need to put my dress on." She sounded more out of breath than she should've been.

"I don't know, that furry thing you have on looks interesting," Scott drawled as he entered. "I particularly like those silver shoes with it." He nudged the door closed with a foot and offered her the flowers.

Hannah took them, inhaling their sweet smell. She smiled. "They're wonderful." She sighed with delight. "Thank you. I love them. Let me get a vase. I'll only be another sec. Have a seat."

When had she become such a chatterer?

"We've plenty of time," he said, chuckling.

He knows he rattles me. I've got to be on guard or I'll be overwhelmed.

In the kitchen, Hannah pulled a chair toward the counter below the cabinet where she stored vases. She removed her shoes. With her robe gathered in her hand, she stepped on the chair, opened the cabinet and reached in for a container.

"Hey, let me help with that." Scott stood beside her. Effortlessly, he grabbed the largest crystal container from the shelf, then closed the cabinet door. The vase clinked as he placed it on the counter.

Scott's gaze dropped to the long expanse of her exposed leg, then lifted to meet hers. Appreciation, heat, and humor warred to dominate, making his eyes darken.

Hannah released her bathrobe, letting it drop to cover her thighs.

Humor won, leaving a twinkle in his eye. "Let me help you down." His hands circled her waist, lifting her. Her hands automatically braced on his shoulders and she could feel muscles bunching beneath the fabric of his suit jacket. She longed to explore their breadth, but resisted the urge.

Their gazes locked, held as she slid at a snail's pace toward the floor. Her toes were inches from touching when he pulled her against his solid frame.

Acutely conscious of her body's reaction to his nearness, Hannah made no effort to be released. Her core heated, glowed, grew brighter and flowed outwards, like a river of lava. Would she burst into flame? Her fingertips kneaded his muscles, asking for something she wouldn't put into words. Scott's quick, heavy breaths mingled with her expectant ones.

The air crackled around them.

For one beautiful, suspended moment Hannah thought he'd kiss her. Hoped he would. Instead, his hands tightened at her waist as he eased her away, letting her feet rest on the floor. Scott stepped back, his hands falling to his sides. Disappointment washed over her. Hannah missed the pleasure of his touch and the promise of his kiss. She shook her head, clearing the cotton-candy fog.

"I'll take care of the flowers. You go get dressed." His words had a rough edge to them, as if he were in pain.

Hurrying across the living room, she closed the bedroom door and let out a soft sigh. Her heart thumped in double time. Darn the man. He didn't seem rattled at all. Would it be considered irony if a heart doctor caused a heart attack?

Keeping her hands off Scott would prove difficult. She'd never responded to another man the same way as she did to him. *That* thrill had been there before, and had returned with a vengeance. She stood stock still. The truth of that reality would mean heartbreak but she was older and wiser now. She'd handle it. Her vow just to remain friends was like a stick that had been thrown into a fast-running river. Long gone.

Hannah slipped her dress over her head. It was the nicest thing she'd ever owned. She'd bought it as a splurge. Had fate known she'd meet Scott again and need it? With a fluttering heart, she took a deep breath. The effort did nothing to calm her anxiousness.

At the mirror, she checked her hair. She'd pulled it into a loose French twist. Tendrils fell to frame her face. Ignoring them, she added a princess strand of pearls to her neck and single pearl studs to her ears.

Taking another fortifying breath, holding it for seconds before letting it go, she stepped out to meet the man that flustered her and sent her heart racing.

* * *

While he waited, Scott wandered the living room, trying to get his libido under control. It was becoming almost impossible to maintain the "just friends" concept between them. Sweat nearly popped out on his brow from the effort he made not to touch Hannah whenever she came near. Taking a deep breath, he tried to focus on something beside the woman dressing a few feet away.

Her condo was small, but adequate for a mother and young child. Floral artwork hung on the walls, adding a bright hominess to the rooms. The furnishings spoke of comfort first, looks second. There was a bit of a backyard where toys of all shapes and colors were strewn. A sandbox was tucked away in the corner. Knowing how Hannah needed space, it was no surprise she'd found a home that would give Jake a place to play.

Framed pictures of Jake and Jake with Hannah rested on tables throughout the room. Scott picked up one where Jake was giving Hannah a kiss on the cheek. Jake looked full of life and Hannah's face held an almost angelic appearance as she smiled with pleasure. It was heartwarming to see such love between a mother and child.

He remembered seeing pictures of his parents

with him and his brothers as small children, but as they'd grown it always seemed his father had been too busy to make time for the family portrait appointment. It wasn't only those his father had missed. The picture taken after Scott's winning run in baseball didn't have his dad in it either.

Scott had tried to understand. He'd known what his father did was important, even admired him. Still, it had hurt when his father hadn't been there for the state baseball play-offs. At first, Scott had thought that if he went into medicine then he would have a connection to his father, but had soon realized that he loved everything about the profession. That, after all, he was his father's son.

He studied the picture of Hannah and Jake again. *What would it be like to be encircled in that glow of emotion?*

He didn't have any business having those kinds of thoughts. He shouldn't be thinking of Hannah in regard to a future. It couldn't include him. He had hurt Hannah before but this time whatever happened between them would also affect Jake. He wouldn't do that to them.

Scott carefully returned the picture to its spot.

Hannah came into the living area. "I'm ready."

Her words tumbled out as she reached for the tiny beaded clutch lying in one of the chairs. With a self-conscious flourish, she faced him.

Scott didn't miss the smallest detail as his eyes took in the amazing vision before him. Hannah must be what angels in heaven look like. Air left his lungs as if he'd been sucker-punched, while his heart rate kicked up ten notches. All his good intentions had fled.

Supported by thin straps at the shoulders, her dress left an expanse of her smooth skin bare. From there the palest of pink fabric fit like a glove across her high breasts, and along her slender waist, to create a cloud of folds that swirled down around her hips and ended an inch above her knees.

He'd never had a lovelier date.

The same rose tint of her dress rested on her checks. She was nervous, self-conscious. A feeling of satisfaction filled him to know that it mattered to her what he thought. He grinned. She refused to meet his gaze. The small jingle of the linked chain of her purse made the lone noise in the room as she wrapped it around her fingers, undid it, and rewrapped it in rapid succession.

His whistle was low and appreciative. "You look amazing."

"Thank you, kind sir. You don't look half bad yourself." Her eyes had a shy look, but her words indicated her confidence was returning. "Shall we go?" She stepped toward the door.

From her head to the tips of her delicate feet, she was perfection. Except for...

He stooped and picked up her thin strapped shoes. They dangled on the ends of two of his fingers. "I believe you might need these." She'd forgotten them when she'd left the kitchen. With a question in her eyes, she looked at him, then down at her feet. He watched with satisfaction as she blushed crimson, making her even more becoming. *She's absolutely captivating.*

Scott liked the strong, demanding Hannah and the give-as-good-as-you-get one, but this sensually unsure Hannah was the best yet. It would be extremely difficult to keep his promise of no pressure when his body was already making demands to have her.

"I guess I do need those." She took the shoes, making an obvious effort not to touch his hand.

Sitting in an armchair, she adjusted the straps around her feet, treating him to a fine expanse of her shapely legs. She caught his appraising stare and pushed her skirt down, effectively closing the curtain on his view. Finding her tiny bag, she stood. "I think I'm ready now."

"I'll have the best-looking woman there on my arm. My colleagues are going to be jealous."

She smiled. The first unwavering one he could remember her having that evening.

"I do believe you're flirting with me, Doctor."

Scott grinned wickedly. "You might be right." He held the door for her. She slipped past him, and Scott had his first view of the back of her dress. From each of her shoulders, the folds of chiffon dropped to scoop below her waist, leaving her back bare.

The rise in his body temperature was instant, probably high enough to break a glass thermometer. He feared he would combust on the spot. *Breathe man, breathe.* His mouth went dry. With effort he remembered to put one foot in front of the other as they went down the walk. All he could think about was placing a kiss on the ridge of one of those golden shoulders while his hand glided along every silky inch of her back.

"That dress is incredible."

"It's not too much for this event, is it?" The insecurity in her voice reminded him of a girl on her first date.

"No, it's perfect, absolutely perfect," he said with almost too much enthusiasm. Taking her hand, he pulled it through the crook of his arm and gave her a broad smile. "And so are you."

She returned the smile with a bright one of her own.

Unaware of her sex appeal, Hannah exuded it with no effort or consciousness. Did she realize his libido was running wild because of her? His body sang in response. His reactions were displaying themselves like a flashing billboard, but she didn't seem to notice. If he didn't focus on keeping the evening light, he could scare her off.

Guiding her to his car, he opened the door and helped her in. The least a mere mortal could do for this celestial being.

Hannah settled into the supple leather seat as Scott maneuvered the low sports car through the late-evening traffic. A tangy smell encircled her. She inhaled, appreciating Scott's own special essence. He smelled like a combination of sun and rain, with a hint of pine. She resisted the yen to lean closer.

"Hey, I'm sorry I gave you a hard time about coming tonight," she said. "It does sounds like a good time, but I'm not sure I'll be much fun. I seem to be unhappy at the hospital and miserable when I'm away. Until Jake gets a heart I'm not sure I'll be satisfied anywhere."

Scott reached for her hand and briefly squeezed it. "Why don't you try not to think about that for a few hours and attempt to enjoy yourself?" He flashed a smile.

One of her favorites. But each of his smiles was jockeying for a spot as favorite. This smile wrapped around her like a blanket on a cold winter day, making her believe that all could be well. A fluttery feeling developed in her stomach. Afraid she might be learning to love more than his smiles, she didn't dare let herself go down that path. "I'll try."

"These events are always laid back and fun. There'll be games, a silent auction, dancing with a good band. We should have no problem finding something distracting to do."

In no time Scott had pulled up in front of a building with massive glass windows. Inside a huge ballroom a band played a fast rock and roll number. Enormous records and pictures of movie stars blown up bigger than life decorated the area. An old '53 Chevy with girls in poodle skirts and guys with slicked-back hair greeted them.

"The fifties. My favorite decade." Hannah smiled, giving Scott's arm a slight press in her enthusiasm. The band struck up the first notes of another song. She swayed to "Earth Angel." With a sheepish grin on her lips, she looked at him from under lowered lashes. "What?"

"I was thinking how appropriate that song is. I've my own earth angel."

Tongue-tied, Hannah could only stare at him.

Scott suppressed a smile...barely. He said close to her ear, "Knowing you, you need to eat before we play."

His lips brushed the shell of her ear, making her body quiver. Her breath caught. Did he have any idea what he did to her? Her stomach did loop-di-loops. She was hungry for more than food.

Scott took her hand. "Let's go and see what's on the buffet."

They wove their way through the crowd towards a group of tables set up on the far side of the room. Her hand fit comfortably into his as if it belonged there. Scott held her hand tight enough to be possessive but not so tight she couldn't have removed it if she'd wished. Her heart missed a beat when he gave it a gentle squeeze, as if he knew what she was thinking.

With their meal completed, Scott took Hannah's hand again as they headed toward an area set up for games. His body needed some type of physical contact with hers, otherwise it felt like a piece of him was missing. He spoke to a couple of his colleagues as he and Hannah walked across the large room. He introduced her only as an old friend, leaving out that she was the mother of one of his patients.

In the game area, they waited their turn after he'd talked Hannah into playing a round of table tennis. He watched her remove the silver shoes, finding the artless action very sexy. Keeping things light was turning into work.

"Did I mention I've been the Watson family reunion champion three years running?" She grinned at him across the expanse of the green table.

"You failed to share that information."

"Don't let that intimidate you."

"I'll try not to." He served his best fast ball.

"Not bad." She nodded with approval. "All

those hours in the interns' hideout in the basement of the hospital must've paid off."

"Just serve, Quinn, and know I'll be giving no mercy."

Hannah grinned, obviously pleased with her efforts to rattle him. At least he'd succeeded in helping her forget her problems for a few minutes.

After a couple of spirited games Scott had a newfound respect for Hannah. She didn't beat him but managed to hold her own.

"You don't feel the need to let my male ego go undamaged by letting me win?" It wasn't a trait he'd normally found in the women he'd been out with.

"No. Why should I? My motto is 'Let the best man or woman win.' Your ego is the last thing I need to feed."

He pulled his lips back in mock pain. "You always did tell me like it is. That's one of the things I always liked about you."

Scott took the final game, barely. Coming around the table, she gave him a quick hug of congratulations. Their laughter merged.

The tinkling sound that he loved placed him hopelessly and completely under her spell. He wanted to hold onto this moment for ever. His days were spent with such serious matters. It was nice to laugh and have fun for a change. Her sharp wit and love of life was infectious.

"That'll show you not to mess with me. That was fun," she said after most of her mirth had dissipated. "I needed to do that. You always could make me laugh. Even when I was having a tough day on the floor," she said. "That's a gift, you know."

"My pleasure." And it was. He always liked her laugh. It reminded him of a breeze moving through wind chimes on a hot summer day. He had an idea she'd not laughed much in the last few years, certainly not in the last few days.

It was nice to see her smiling, letting go a little. She needed to. Her emotions had to be swinging one way and then the other. She needed a release.

"What?" she asked, sounding a little ill at ease.

"I was just contemplating what an interesting woman you are."

"How's that?"

"Well, you play table tennis like a demon, love donuts, you're evidently a self-sufficient single mother, you appreciate nice cars and you like the oldies."

Scott noticed the worry lines on her face had decreased. For that he was grateful. She had looks that went beyond attractive. Hers was still a wholesome beauty, the kind of loveliness that came from the inside. The type that had drawn him to her in the first place, making him want to get to know her, and later to consider the impossible.

Turning her shoulder in a saucy manner toward him, she said, "What more could a man want?"

"I can imagine."

She immediately flushed red, making her even more desirable.

"Don't be using that charm on me, Doctor. It won't work. I've seen it in action too many times. That's just a figure of speech."

He chuckled. "Yes, Hannah, I know what you meant." It was nice to see that some of the spunk that had attracted him when they'd first met hadn't disappeared. His plan was working. He'd been right to insist she accompany him. She needed fun in her life. If he could, he would have it be that way for her always.

"I'm thirsty." Her eyes shined as she smiled.

"Then let's get you something to drink." He hoped none of his colleagues saw the sappy grin on his face. He could imagine the unmerciful fun they would make of him. The grapevine would no doubt run with that information. "Don't forget your shoes."

Hannah found them under the playing table and slipped them on.

"I think it adds something to your dress when you're barefooted." Hannah's nervous laughter sent heat to a part of his body that didn't need any encouragement. "Come on, hotshot, I think there's a soda stand over this way." He pointed to a red and white awning.

As they made their way across the room, Hannah exclaimed, "I thought you meant a place to get a cola! This is a real soda parlor."

They found a small empty table. A young man, dressed in a yellow striped shirt, took their order. She wanted a chocolate shake. He ordered vanilla.

"I'm really enjoying myself." Hannah's eyes sparkled. "There must be thousands of nurses wishing you'd invited them."

"I think it is more like a hundred." He gave what he hoped was his best wolfish grin.

She laughed. "At least."

The young man returned with their shakes.

Hannah stuck her straw into hers. Her cheeks drew together as she sucked. A look of pure joy touched her features as she drew up the rich liquid. He grinned. Releasing the straw, she ran her tongue with slow deliberation across the curve of her top lip. Closing her eyes, she made a sound of unadulterated pleasure.

Had all the air been sucked out of the place? Scott couldn't breathe. Captured by the sight, he wished he'd been the one to put that look of delight on her face.

Hannah's smiled broadened. "I'll race you to the bottom. On your mark, get set, go."

He shoved his straw into his glass. The thick liquid moved up their straws at a slow pace. Watching her over the top of the glass, Scott raised a brow, taunting her. Smirking around the straw, he continued to suck hard.

"You won't beat me." Determination filled her eyes as her lips drew on the straw again.

Scott put his hand under the table and caressed her knee. Hannah's eyes widened in surprise, then narrowed. He beamed. She shoved his hand away and moved her knee to where he couldn't touch her with ease. With a negative movement of her head and a gleam in her eye, she continued sucking with gusto.

He broke contact with his straw and let out a laugh that came from his belly. It was loud enough that others sitting around them stared. The last noisy slurp of nothing being left in her glass could be heard by the time his mirth had died into a chuckle.

"I won." Hannah clasped her hands over her head in a victory sign. "And you tried to cheat!"

Scott laughed again, feeling no guilt. "Yeah. In the end you got the better of me. I could tell that, no matter what I did, you planned to win this contest."

"You're right." Hannah grinned. "We should've set a prize."

"How about this?" Not allowing her time to answer or caring if he was seen, Scott slipped a hand behind her neck and pulled her to him.

Her lips were cool under his. In a slow, methodical motion his tongue slid over her lips, not wanting to miss any of the sugary flavor. Hannah brought her hand to his shoulder and made a low sound of acceptance. Her mouth heated under his. Long, perfect seconds went by before he lifted his mouth.

CHAPTER SIX

SCOTT'S hooded eyes and the sensual curve of his lips made Hannah's blood speed through her veins. A blur of shapes and colors whirled around them. Scott was the only person who remained in focus.

Her gaze locked with his blue one. The air snapped round them. He leaned toward her. Her lips parted.

A man moving between the tables jostled Scott's chair. Pulling back, Scott sat straighter. The moment evaporated. He'd been thinking about kissing her again. She would've let him.

"I think, no, I know, kissing you could get out of hand and I promised no pressure."

As far as Hannah was concerned, he could forget that pledge. She wanted him and she wanted to feel wanted. Even if it was just for a little while.

"There's a silent auction going on. I read a trip down the Colorado River through the Grand

Canyon was being offered. I'd like to bid on it.
After we check that out, maybe we could dance,
if you'd like," he said, standing.

Scott sounded a little formal all of a sudden.
The abrupt shift in his attitude made her feel a
little lost. He'd been so warm minutes before.
Had that kiss affected him as much as it had her?

Lifting a finger, Hannah touched her bottom
lip. She should be grateful for the interruption.
It gave her time to get her emotions corralled.

As they strolled side by side toward the auction area, she noticed the number of admiring
looks that came Scott's way from other women.
Hannah glowed with feminine one-upmanship,
knowing he was with her.

The area where the auction was set up was quieter. A few other couples strolled around the tables. Scott located the Canyon trip and wrote his
bid on the sheet. Hannah coughed to cover her
gasp of shock when she saw his bid amount.

He must've known what she thought because
he said, "It's for a good cause."

"Yours or the hospital's?" she asked with a grin.

"Both."

Hannah realized he could afford it. A reminder
of how different their worlds were.

They continued down the line of tables filled with auction items. An exquisite blue floral tea-set caught Hannah's eye. Picking up the cup, she checked the bottom to find it had been made by a quality British company. She ran the tip of her index finger along the scalloped rim of the fragile cup. Returning it to the matching saucer, she lifted the pair to admire what a beautiful pair they made.

"It's beautiful." She spoke more to herself than Scott. The magnificent set was one she'd enjoy owning and using.

"Would you like to bid on it?" Scott asked from behind her.

She'd been so engrossed in admiring the set she'd not seen Scott put down an autographed baseball and join her.

"No. No. I was just looking." Even the starting bid was way beyond what she could afford.

"I'd be glad to bid for you." Scott studied the auction sheet.

"No. I don't even have a good place to put it," she assured him. "And I've a small child. Nothing like this would survive long in my home."

"You're probably right. How about a dance now

or would you rather play some more games? I could let you win this time."

"Funny. It's not a real win unless you earn it." She looked at him. "But let's go and see if you're as good on the dance floor as you are at table tennis."

He draped her arm through his. She'd noticed he'd made a point all night not to touch her back. During the last few days she had especially liked him placing his hand at the small of her back, like an old-world gentleman. Why wouldn't he touch her back now?

The music became louder as they approached the tile-covered dance floor.

"I wonder if my *must-attend* cotillion lessons when I was thirteen will stand up to this." His lips curve into a boyish smile.

"You'll be better than me. My skills come from dancing in the living room with my father. Most of the time on his feet."

"As a kid I use to watch my dad swirl and twirl my mom around the house. Mother always wanted my father to take her dancing. She loved to dance. Still does."

"That's a nice memory."

He didn't say anything for a second, as if he'd

never thought of it like that before. "You know, it is. Come on, let's give it a shot. What do you say?"

"Lead on, Mr. Astaire." She beamed up at him.

Scott placed his hand low, but not too low, on her back. Hannah's breath jerked to a stop for a second. Heat radiated out from where his hand moved over her skin. Maybe it'd been a good idea for him not to touch her. It'd been a long time since she'd allowed an adult male's interest.

He maneuvered them across the floor to where other couples were preparing to dance. A fast tune began. It took a few steps for Hannah to adjust to Scott's closeness and the rhythm of the music. She settled into his lead. He was an excellent dancer. With his lithe and athletic body, he moved across the floor with natural grace. Scott twisted her in his arms, spun her one way then another and even dipped her following one number.

"How about a cold drink?" he asked after a set of songs. She nodded her agreement and he took her hand, leading her off the dance floor.

"Please. This is the most exercise I've had in days," she said, breathless from exertion and being in his arms. "I should've known when you suggested dancing you would be good at it."

Scott found a cart selling sodas, and then they located a spot out of the way where they could sit.

"Thanks," she said when he handed her the drink. "I thought you said you didn't dance well."

"No, what I said was it'd been some time." He smiled down at her. "I'm rusty at it. I don't have much spare time to go dancing."

"You're still a great partner. Mr. Astaire wouldn't be disappointed in you."

"Thank you, ma'am." He gave her a regal nod. "As are you." He took a swallow of his drink. "I was wondering why I never took you dancing."

"I wouldn't go out with you, remember? I saw you for the womanizer you were." She grinned at him. "Anyway, if we'd gone out it would've ruined a friendship. I wanted more than a date. What happen between us proved I was right."

"I see your point. I'm sorry. I handled things badly." His words seemed to include more than not taking her on a date.

"You can stop apologizing. I've grown up. Moved on. I have Jake to be concerned about. Men that come into my life affect him too. It's not just me getting hurt any more, it's Jake too."

"You're a strong woman."

"I don't know about that. I'm simply a mother doing the best she can for her child. He has no one else but me." She took a swig of her drink, and put her cup down.

He nodded in understanding. Slipping his hand in his pocket, he pulled out his cell phone and handed it to her. "Here, why don't you call and check on him? The hospital is number one on speed dial."

"I'm not surprised." His eyes clouded over for a second. Had she said something wrong?

"I would be paged if there was a problem, but I know you wouldn't be happy unless you heard he was fine from the nurse."

"You know me so well."

"Not as well as I would like to." His voice took on a suggestive note. Time held still between them then he said, "You go find someplace quiet enough to check on Jake, and I'll go and have a look at how the silent auction is going. I'll meet you back here by Elvis."

"I won't be long," she said over her shoulder as she walked away.

Ten minutes later they were both standing beside the life-size Elvis cutout.

"How's Jake?" Scott asked as she joined him.

"Resting. And I know you want to say I told you so but please don't."

"You're a great mom. I see a lot of mothers who shouldn't have the job. It's nice to see a parent who has a connection to their child. Sadly, it doesn't always happen."

"Thank you. Sometimes I think I'm fumbling around in the dark."

"You're more in the daylight than you know." A slow song began and the lights dimmed above the dance floor. "Would you like to see some of my best moves?" he asked, his voice going low. He led her into the center of the already overflowing floor.

"I can't imagine them being any better than what I've already experienced."

Gathering her into his arms, Scott placed a hand on her back. She couldn't help but tense at the stimulating contact, but soon relaxed enough to lean into him. One of her hands found his and the other slid along his arm to rest at his shoulder. When another couple bumped them, Scott flexed his arm at her waist bringing her closer.

The solidness of his body met hers from head to toe. Hannah had a sense of being protected from the ugliness of the world. His hand dipped low on her waist before it moved inch by tantalizing inch up the length of her spine to her neck. A hot trail of consciousness flowed through her as his fingers paused at each dip in her vertebrae then worked his way down again. She simmered in the heat his touch created in her. His hand came to rest in the bow of her back.

His lips touched the sensitive spot behind her ear, sending a jolt of awareness rocketing through her.

"Scott..."

"Shh, let me enjoy having you in my arms."

Hannah's hand gripped his upper arm. Every fiber of her being strained toward him, hyper-responsive to each nuance of Scott's touch. His chest rose and fell against hers. When his heartbeat increased, she felt it. Skimming her hand over his shoulder, she curled her fingers into the waves of hair at the nape of his neck. Stepping closer, she breathed deeply, taking him in. A soft sound of pure pleasure escaped.

Scott groaned, pulling her tighter. His thigh slipped between her legs as they swayed slowly to the music. Scott no longer led to the beat of the music, but to his personal one.

His fingertips followed the edge of her dress along her back until his hand came to rest in the folds. He slowly slipped his fingers under the material to settle near the curve of her breast.

A tingle ran through her. Her nipples strained upward, pebble hard. Her step faltered. Scott compensated with a flawless move, holding her snug against his length, his desire hard against her belly.

His pager vibrated between them, bursting the blissful, sensual balloon they'd been floating in.

He expelled a scalding word and eased his hold.

Her body throbbed with need left unmet.

Scott unclipped the phone from his waistband, glanced at the screen, then muttered a blunt curse under his breath.

Hannah put more space between them. "Is it about Jake? Is something wrong?" she asked, fear filling her voice.

"I don't know yet, honey. Let me answer this." His voice was husky with disappointment. He led her off the dance floor and into a quieter area.

"This is McIntyre," he said sharply into his phone. "Yes. Can you see to it? Yes. That sounds good." His manner had turned all business.

She put a hand on his arm, and caught his gaze. "Jake?" She whispered the plea.

Scott put his hand over the receiver and mouthed, "He's fine, honey," before continuing his conversation.

Hannah took a deep breath and released it, listening to the low rumble of Scott's voice. If the call had come an hour later they would've been making love. She would've been a willing partner. Very willing. The tornado of sensations still swirled through her. Scott had set her on fire. She'd never before experienced the all-consuming need he elicited from her.

Now he stood discussing a patient. His mood had shifted lightning quick. She'd been forgotten. He'd morphed into doctor mode. But with something as simple as catching her hand, she'd be lost again.

Her feelings overpowered all logical thought, shocking her. Maintain control, that's what she needed to do. Think first. Not to expect more than Scott could give. None of that mattered. Scott had already left his mark.

Hannah watched as his jaw tightened and he looked off into the distance. His questions came out short and succinct.

As if he suddenly remembered she was there, Scott reached for her hand and pulled her close, wrapping an arm around her waist. Already her plan had a huge hole in it. She couldn't control Scott. The heat from his body surrounded her.

"I'll be there within the hour." He flipped his cell phone closed, and turned her so she could look at him.

"Something has come up that will require our attention. He curved his lip into a confident smile. "We think we've found a heart for Jake."

"Oh, thank God."

He squeezed her shoulders. "Now, remember we're in the beginning stage, and it'll take hours before we know for sure, but the heart looks promising."

"Please let this be the one," she whispered.

"I'm going straight to the hospital to review the information about the possible donor and check on Jake. Timing is everything now."

"I'll go with you."

"No," he said firmly, "you don't need to be sitting and fretting at the hospital. I'll drop you at my place. That way you'll be close. It could be hours before I know more. I'll call you."

She refused to let him dictate whether or not

she should be there for her child. "I'm going with you. Jake's my son and I want to be with him as much as I can. Anyway, I have a change of clothes at the hospital and a sleep room in my name. It makes more sense."

He nodded his agreement but didn't appear happy about the arrangements.

In a hurry, Scott left her where the hallway divided, one hallway going to CICU and the other to the waiting room. She missed the security he represented the second he was out of sight.

With Scott gone, Hannah stood in the middle of the corridor, suddenly unsure what to do next. She couldn't move. This was it, what she'd prayed for. Only she'd never have dreamed she'd be involved emotionally with the doctor who would be saving Jake's life. She'd stopped thinking straight the minute Scott had arrived earlier that evening. With the possibility of a heart for Jake, the situation had become more desperate.

Change. That's what she needed to do. She rode the elevator to the upper floor and found the small sleep room she'd been assigned that afternoon. She'd made arrangements for it so she wouldn't be tempted to stay at Scott's. The room held a single bed and end table. It wasn't much, but it was close to Jake. Withdrawing her bag from the locker where she'd stored it earlier, she dropped it on the bed and began to change.

A flood of heat washed over her as she removed her dress. She overflowed with longing. If it hadn't been for the tremors of Scott's pager she'd no doubt be in his bed right now. Her heart rate quickened. A flood of hunger washed over her as if Scott was near.

She couldn't deny she'd been as willing a participant as he. No way could she place all the blame on him.

Pulling a pair of comfortable jeans out of the bag, she slipped them on, added a favorite T-shirt and tennis shoes, grabbed a sweatshirt, and hurried out to check on Jake.

"Mrs. Quinn wants to come back. Is that okay?" the clerk asked the midnight shift nurse.

Scott, standing by the desk, looked up from the chart he'd been reviewing. He'd asked her to wait. It figured she wouldn't listen. Hannah had certainly never been intimidated by him. The nurse looked at him and he nodded his consent.

The clerk had hardly replaced the phone receiver before Hannah entered the unit. She glanced at him but continued straight to Jake's bed.

Scott appreciated the view of Hannah's shapely backside as she stretched and leaned over the rail of the bed to place a kiss on her sleeping son's head. He needed to get his thoughts off the mom and on the son.

To give her some time alone with Jake, Scott waited before he approached. "Hannah." The word came out sharper than he'd intended. Lowering his voice to a more mellow level, Scott said, "I told you to wait until I came to get you."

Hannah glared at him. "I couldn't wait." She turned back to Jake. "I had to see him." Her voice caught. She was in protective mode.

"You're right." Scott understood her feelings because he felt that same need to protect her. He admired her strength. There was no begging and pleading or demands on her part. She just did what had to be done because she loved her child.

The desire to wrap her in his arms pulled at him, but he would have an audience. The best he could offer, though inadequate, was the reassurance of knowing what she could expect in the next few hours. He moved to the other side of the bed in order to put some space between them. Hannah had a way of making him do things he'd not planned to whenever she was within touching distance.

She looked at him in expectation with a gleam of moisture in her eyes. Her hand clasped one of Jake's.

"Let me explain what's happening and going to happen. Right now, we're waiting on the family of the possible donor to agree to donation. Most of the time the recipient family never knows this far in advance about a possible donor."

"You get to know sooner if you're out dancing with the surgeon," Hannah said, averting her eyes.

His lips became a thin line. The acute sting of the remark registered.

Hannah brought her eyes back to his. "I'm sorry. That was uncalled for."

Glancing to see if anyone watched, Scott reached across the bed and captured one of her hands. His thumb brushed over her knuckles before he released it. "I understand, but don't regret what almost happened between us. I certainly don't."

She gave him a wry smile.

"As I was saying, the family will have to agree, which will probably take place in the morning. Afterwards there'll be more tests, and it may not be until tomorrow…" he looked at his watch "…or I mean this afternoon, before things will really start moving along. The thoracic fellow will go after the heart. I plan to stay here with Jake. He won't go into surgery until after the fellow has left. We'll be in constant contact until the fellow walks into the OR with Jake's new heart."

"Will I know what's happening?"

"Yes. Andrea will be coming into the OR and I'll be sending messages out to you."

"So nothing may happen until tomorrow evening?"

He nodded. "That's why I insisted you didn't need to be here."

"I couldn't stay away."

"I realize that now. It's just part of who you are. If I hadn't had my mind on other matters I might've been thinking more clearly."

Even in the dim light he could see her blush. She knew exactly what he'd been referring to.

"So why don't you go up and try to get some rest? I'll call you when there's something new to tell. I'm even going to bunk in the attending's room for a few hours so I'll be ready for surgery."

"You don't have to stay right here?"

"No, they'll call me with any questions. We're good at transplants here, Hannah. My staff knows their jobs and they do them well."

"Dr. Mac, Lifeline is on the phone," the clerk called, holding the phone out.

Hannah spun around to look at the nurse.

Scott circled the bed, stopped beside her and said, "Wait for me outside the unit. This call shouldn't take long. I'll walk you to the elevator." He made a few steps and stopped, turning back to her. "Please wait," he pleaded softly. "Jake is hopefully going to have his new heart soon."

Hannah kissed her sleeping child, wishing she could hug him close, and left the unit. She lingered outside the CICU doors. "Still thinking of me?" Scott quipped as he came out, a slight grin on his lips.

He was obviously trying to add some levity to this anxious and unsure time. "Mighty confident of yourself, aren't you?" Her smile grew, despite her effort to control it.

His grin disappeared and his look turned solemn. "Not where you're concerned."

Scott's intense gaze bored into hers for a long moment before he took her arm and directed her down the corridor. They walked in silence, with uneasiness hanging between them. At the elevator Hannah pushed the "up" button.

"I want to kiss you." Scott's words were a husky demand.

Hannah's body tingled. Her pulse pounded. Her fingers itched to touch him. "I...I...don't think that's a good idea. I think we both should focus on Jake."

Scott stepped away, his jaw tight. "Jake will be getting my very best care. In no way will I let what I feel for you affect my performance as a doctor."

"I didn't mean to imply—"

"Hannah, I know you're beating yourself up over what was happening between us on the dance floor. I wish you wouldn't. I know all the negatives to this relationship. You still don't completely trust me and I understand. I can't make you any promises, but I also know there's something special between us."

She remained silent. There was something amazing between them. She felt it too. But she needed to be sure about her next move. She'd misread him before, had completely missed the mark with her husband, and she couldn't afford to do it again. Scott had convinced her to trust him with Jake's heart but she still didn't know about hers.

"Try to get some sleep. I'll call you as soon as I know something more concrete."

Scott turned, going back toward the unit. She'd wanted him as much as he'd wanted her. Scott wanted her sexually, but she was looking for someone to share her future. He hadn't been willing to do that during medical school. Could he feel differently now? If she invested her heart, she had to know he wanted the same things in life she did. She owed it to Jake, and to herself.

The trouble was, she was weak around Scott, and so very alone.

In the hospital the next morning, Hannah's cell phone hadn't completed a full note before she snatched it up. Her heart jumped when she heard Scott's voice.

"Hannah, we think this is the heart for Jake." His tone sounded professional, somber. "But it'll be hours before we'll go to collect it. Jake's resting and everything looks good on the donor end."

"Thank goodness." She closed her eyes and said a silent prayer.

"I'm sorry I can't tell you more. I'll see you later. I've gotta go."

His abrupt end to the conversation startled her. She wasn't sure she appreciated the return of his all-business manner. She'd come to enjoy, anticipate, the warmer version. It had become part of her comfort zone.

Despite her jumbled emotions, the chain of events leading to Jake getting a new heart registered. On a human *and* parental level she knew another family had lost their child in order for hers to live. Her chest constricted. As wonderful as Jake getting another chance to live was for her, at the other end of the spectrum was the donor family's devastation. Moisture blurred her vision. The thought of what those parents must be feeling was almost impossible to endure. Their two families would be forever linked.

Clutching a pillow, she caught herself wishing for the security of Scott's arms. He'd really been wonderful and supportive, not only with her but with Jake. She had to admit she'd felt a twinge of jealousy when Scott had managed to get Jake to laugh. She hadn't been able to do that. Wiping tears away, she took a fortifying breath. There were things to do, calls to make.

Phoning her sister in California, Hannah told her about the available heart. Despite the distance, Hannah felt better just talking to her. Jake was getting a new heart. She could scarcely comprehend it.

Scott managed to get a few hours of sleep at the hospital between calls from Lifeline and thoughts of Hannah creeping into his dreams. The long hours leading up to a transplant were often tedious. Reviewing the donor's history, checking the heart size to see if it would fit into the chest cavity and assessing blood work were a few of the many details he'd organized that morning.

A heart transplant took careful and well-timed actions. An amazing life-and-death dance. It never ceased to fill him with awe that he had a part in something so phenomenal.

Dancing. For ever after, dancing would be synonymous with Hannah. He loved holding her, wanted her in his arms again. Soon. It had hurt when she had refused to kiss him at the elevator, but she'd made the right call. They needed to take things slower.

They were on two different paths. Her life was hearth and home, and he couldn't commit to that. He wasn't capable of giving Jake and Hannah what they needed or deserved. It would be another failed relationship to add to his list.

The life he'd chosen made it impossible for him to be doctor and family man. He couldn't foresee doing both well. He already carried the heavy weight of guilt from letting his work get in the way when his mother had needed him. Hurting Hannah or Jake was something he wasn't prepared to accept. Some people could manage different parts of their life effectively, but he couldn't. The McIntyre family history bore that out.

He was just too much like his father. His patients had always come first, and Scott felt the same way about the children he cared for. That the idea he and Hannah could have more even crossed his mind came as a surprise.

It would be late evening or early morning before the major part of his day would be complete. Now wasn't the time to consider what-ifs.

Scott looked up to see Hannah coming through the CICU doors. He met her beside Jake's bed.

Jake's eyelids opened a moment and then slid closed again.

"I've ordered something to make him sleep. Jake needs to be well rested before going into surgery," Scott said. "Did you get any sleep?"

He stood close enough to catch a whiff of the fresh apple smell of her hair when she turned to him. Scott ached to pull her into a dark corner and kiss her until her cool demeanor fell away. Until the hot passion he knew she held in check boiled over.

"Some," Hannah said, before taking Jake's hand. "Is there any news?" she asked, her attention totally focused on her son.

"Yes. The family has agreed to donate. Now Lifeline has to see that all the organs being donated are placed before the retrievals."

"All the organs?"

"Yeah. The family can agree to give other organs."

"Other children will share the same donor as Jake?"

"They could. Depending on what organs the family agrees to donate. I think we'll be going after the heart around six this evening." Scott forced his voice to remain flat, showing none of the concern he felt about the upcoming surgery. He'd grown attached to the little boy. This would be one surgery where he couldn't leave his feelings at the door.

"Where's the heart coming from?"

"I can't say, but not too far away. A heart has to be transplanted within four hours so that doesn't let it travel a long distance."

Hannah nodded, and he watched her thick hair bounce around her shoulders. His fingers flexed and curled in an effort to keep him from succumbing to his longing to touch it.

They stood by Jake's bed, doing nothing more than watching her sleeping boy. Scott practiced equal care and concern for all his patients, but this particular little patient had become a personal case despite his efforts not to let it happen. He wanted to save Jake's life. He must.

"It won't be long now," he said with all the confidence he possessed.

"Mrs. Quinn?" Andrea placed a light touch on Hannah's arm long hours later.

Hannah blinked. "What?"

"It's time to get Jake ready to go down. You need to say goodbye to him." Compassion filled her voice. It held something encouraging in it, maybe a note of excitement. "He's going now?"

Jake needed the transplant, but it was difficult to let him go. At least now he was alive. He might not live though surgery. The known was better than the unknown. The terror of losing Jake filled Hannah's body like a sharp wind on a bitter winter morning.

"No. He'll actually go down in about an hour. It takes a while to prep him," Andrea said.

Hannah tensed. A film of wetness blurred her view. She needed to absorb him, afraid this would be her last memory. Studying every detail of Jake's precious face, she wanted to remember him happy and smiling, laughing with Scott…

Stop. She inhaled, letting the breath out in measured puffs. Jake had to live.

Sedated and on a respirator, her precious son had no idea what was happening. Jake lay pale against the white sheets of the bed, the only color in his face being the dark circles under his eyes. She wanted to drop to her knees and cry, howl at how unfair it all was.

"I love you, honey. Be strong. See you soon." Kissing his cheek, she released his tiny hand and cringed when it fell limply on the bed. She refused to use the word *goodbye*.

Jake would be fine. She'd accept nothing less. She believed Scott would allow nothing less.

"Mrs. Quinn," Andrea said in a low, gentle voice. "They're expecting him in the OR. Why don't you go on down to the surgery waiting room? Do you know where it is?"

"Yes." The word came out as a croak.

"Good. I'll be down to join you in a little while."

Hannah balanced on her toes, leaned over the rail and placed a kiss on Jake's forehead. A tear dropped onto his face. Hannah wiped it away. "I love you, sweetie."

Andrea put a hand on her shoulder. The comfort was appreciated. "I'll tell Scott where you are. He'll want to talk to you before going into the OR." Hannah wiped her cheek with the back of her hand as she made the long, lonely walk to the waiting room.

Her chest tightened. Would she be able to draw another complete breath until Jake came out of surgery?

Be positive. Straighten up. Jake will be fine.

Taking a seat in the far corner of the waiting room, Hannah settled in for the night. A few minutes later Andrea entered and took a seat close by.

"You'll see a big difference in Jake right away," Andrea said.

Hannah appreciated Andrea trying to make conversation while at the same time she just wanted to be left alone. "That's what the nurses tell me."

Scott came through the door dressed in blue scrubs with his ever-present white lab coat. Hannah stood, meeting him in the center of the room. If he'd opened his arms, she wouldn't have thrown herself into them, but he didn't.

Instead he said, "Let's sit. We need to talk." He placed his hands lightly at her waist, turning her. Hannah wanted to lean into his strength, but found her chair again as directed. Scott sat in the one beside her, which put Hannah between him and Andrea.

He took her hand. Desperate for his offered comfort, she didn't pull away. Looking into her eyes, he promised, "I'll take good care of Jake."

"I know you will," Hannah whispered, making her trust evident.

"Jake's getting settled in surgery. He's had his first dose of Prograf, which is the antirejection medicine. The team going after the heart has been gone almost an hour. I'll be in touch with them at regular intervals until they return. As close as I can to the heart's arrival, I'll open Jake's chest."

Hannah winced. He shifted closer, giving her hand a squeeze.

"You need to understand this is an iffy process right up until the new heart gets to the OR. Something could happen to the heart, the time could go too long, or we might find out at the last minute that the heart isn't good enough. There's a chance we may not be able to do it tonight."

She looked at him, saying nothing, praying, *Oh, God, please let it be tonight.*

Scott tightened his hold on her hand. "Surgery will probably take around four to six hours. Don't expect to see me any time soon. I'll be out when Jake's ready to go up to the unit."

He glanced at Andrea. Standing, he pulled Hannah into his arms. Hers went around his waist, absorbing his warmth, strength and assurance. His confidence and support was like balm to her nerves.

Scott ran his hand over her back, making no

move to leave. He brushed his lips across her temple, then released her.

Hannah gripped his upper arms. Tears, swimming in her eyes, blurred his handsome face. She silently begged him to tell her that everything would be okay.

Scott's hand cupped her cheek and he looked directly into her eyes for an extended moment before he said, "Next time you see me, Jake will have his new heart."

CHAPTER SEVEN

SCOTT stood at the surgery wash basin, running a small white brush beneath his fingernails. The antibacterial soap formed froth.

He'd performed numerous heart transplants. Being well trained, he knew what to expect. Yet he hadn't been this nervous since his first surgery.

It added pressure to an already hyper-sensitive situation. Why hadn't he at least waited until Jake was out of the hospital to get to know Hannah better?

He'd tried to resist her, but it seemed like he was always there when she needed help. Touching her had become addictive. He didn't understand this unfamiliar emotion. She'd slid his world sideways.

His heart had soared when Hannah had said she trusted him. Looking in the mirror above the basin, he saw the amazed look on his face. He loved Hannah.

Scott stood shock still. Muttering an inappropriate word for a children's hospital, Scott's foot slipped off the water control, stopping the flow over his hands. How had he let this happen?

What was he going to do? He couldn't act on that emotion. He refused to. Loving someone meant making them happy, and he could never make Hannah happy.

Pain squeezed his heart. He'd never be really happy without her. She'd become his world. But he would never tell her so.

The surgery nurse next to him cleared her throat, drawing his attention. She handed him a sterile towel.

There was no time or energy to waste dwelling on the revelation. His needed to focus on Jake getting his new heart.

Another nurse helped him into gloves before he shouldered through the door of OR Four. The coolness of the room surrounded him. He'd soon be grateful for the lower temperature. It not only kept the heat from the operating lights reasonable, but helped slow the patient's blood flow. Right now he was glad to have the cold bring his mind back to the job at hand. He knew this routine. Understood this world. He had control here.

Jake lay on the operating table with his hands

held securely and under sterile drapes. Scott didn't make a habit of viewing a patient, but he couldn't help but look at Jake. The boy's soft laugh as he himself had made animal noises came to his mind. He touched one of Jake's hands briefly. Like a punch in the stomach, the realization came that he'd fallen for this little guy as well.

This surgery *must* go well.

The anesthesiologist sedating Jake sat at his head. "Mac, are you okay?"

Scott nodded. He had to get in the zone and let his training take over from his emotions. Jake's life was in his hands. "Is everyone ready?" he asked. The smell of sterilizing solution wafted through the brightly lit OR.

The phone on the wall rang.

"Heart's on its way. It looks good. It should be here in two hours. They'll call back when they're in the air," the nurse announced.

Flipping down the small but intense light stationed between surgical magnifying glasses, Scott stated, "Let's get the chest open and this young man on bypass. Scalpel."

He made an incision down the center of the

chest, opening it. The heart looked exactly as he'd told Hannah it would. Large and flabby.

"Needs a new one," one of the assisting fellows remarked from across the table.

"Let's see that he gets it." Scott glanced at the clock.

The shrill ring of the phone drew his attention. The team was in the air. Forty minutes away. No time to waste.

"Let's get him on bypass," Scott stated.

Minutes later the swishing and bumping of the heart-lung machine became a constant sound in the room.

The phone rang again.

"The helicopter's on the roof. The heart's on its way down," the nurse said.

"We're ready." Scott concentrated on his patient.

Minutes later the door swung open and a two-man team entered with the new heart. One man carried a small white cooler. On top, printed in red, were the words "Live Organ."

Looking at the heart with care, Scott said, "Looks good. Time?"

"Two hours, eighteen minutes."

Great. He had leeway. He'd have time to get the heart into its new home and some to spare.

"Scalpel." With skilled precision, Scott removed Jake's damaged heart and replaced it with the donated one. "Nice fit. Sutures."

The new heart looked wonderful. Strong. Healthy. The tests indicated the match was a good one but, still, you never really knew for sure until the heart was in place if the body would accept it. The match needed to be good enough Jake wouldn't have any major problems with rejection but there were never any guarantees. Despite medical advances, heart transplants were still medical miracles.

"Coming off bypass."

The rhythmic sound of the heart-lung machine ceased as the transplant team stood around Jake, holding a unified breath.

"Releasing the clamps," the fellow said.

Blood flowed through the new heart.

It quivered.

It shifted.

With a jerk, it began to beat.

Scott always felt a sense of awe when he watched a transplanted heart begin beating on its own. It took a few seconds before the heart moved into a steady pace of thump…bump…thump…

Surgery couldn't have gone more textbook perfect. Scott felt like a weight had been lifted off his shoulders.

"Andrea, you can let Hannah…uh…Mrs. Quinn know that the heart is in and looks great. Jake is stable."

Hannah saw the smile on Andrea's face as she came through the waiting-room door. She could tell the woman had good news and Andrea's words confirmed her confidence in Scott.

"Thank God," she cried in relief, as joy bubbled up and escaped.

She hugged Andrea. "What happens now?"

"Scott will watch closely for bleeding and then close." Her tone was reserved, but she wore a smile.

"How long will that take?"

"If all goes well, about an hour." Her look turned more serious. "We still have some hurdles to get over. Jake's not out of the woods yet."

Hannah sank into a chair, her knees going weak. *Jake has a new heart.*

With an impatient clasping and unclasping of

hands, Hannah stared at the waiting-room door, then glanced at the clock on the wall. An hour had passed. Where was Scott? Was something wrong? Why didn't he come?

As soon as Scott entered the waiting room, Hannah jumped up. He grinned at her. *Jake was doing well.* In her happiness, Hannah wrapped her arms around Scott's neck. He felt solid and secure, safe. Scott pulled Hannah close, lifting her off her feet.

"Oh, Scott..." she whispered into his neck. "Thank you, thank you, thank you." He lowered her, letting her feet touch the floor. Taking her hand, he led her to a chair, indicating she should sit. He sat in the chair next to hers.

"How's Jake?"

"He's doing as well as can be expected." Scott gave her hand a reassuring squeeze. "I wanted to explain what'll happen next."

Andrea rose. "I'll let you two talk."

"Thanks," Scott said. "For everything."

"No problem, Mac. I'll be back in a few minutes to walk up to the unit with Hannah."

Scott gave Andrea an appreciative smile. "I owe you one."

She smiled. "Glad to be of help." Andrea went out the door.

Hannah's attention returned to Scott. "What was that about?"

"I asked her to sit with you during surgery. I didn't want you to be alone."

She gave him a grateful smile. "I'm glad you did. It was a long night and would've been even longer sitting here by myself." She scooted closer. "Now, tell me about Jake."

After taking both her hands in his, Scott said, "Jake did well through the surgery. The new heart looks great." He absently played with her fingers as he spoke. "The heart even started on its own, which is always a good sign. He's in CICU now. You can see him after he's settled. The plan is for him to be in the unit for three days, then be moved to the cardiac step-down unit."

Hannah sighed. "I can't wait." Some of her fear and worry fell away. "I'll get to hold him again. Take care of him."

Scott stood, and pulled her up beside him.

Slipping her arms around his waist, Hannah lifted her gaze to his. "I can't thank you enough," she said pouring all the gratitude she felt into the words.

He looked deep into her eyes and returned her hug. "You're welcome. You have to remember, Jake isn't out of the woods yet. He has to come off the respirator and be moved to the step-down unit before he's well enough to go home. There's rejection to be concerned about and med adjustments to be made."

Hannah refused to let her happiness be dampened. "I understand, but getting the heart was a giant step. He'll make it through the rest. I just know he'll be all right."

"That's what we're working towards." Scott followed the line of her cheek with the tip of his index finger. "I love your spirit."

At the insistent buzzing of Scott's pager Hannah moved away but remained in his arms. She was close enough to read 911 Quinn on the pager screen.

At Scott's look of alarm, her stomach dropped, and rolled. She clutched his arm. "Something's happen to Jake."

Scott pushed her away and set her in a chair. "I have to go."

Andrea returned as he rushed out the door. "Take care of Hannah," he called over his shoulder.

Scott ran along the hallway, took the stairs two

steps at a time, ran down another corridor and shoved through the unit doors.

Oh, God. This can't be happening. Not to Jake.

His bed was already surrounded by staff working at a fast but efficient speed.

Frantic, Scott made his way into the thick of things. His heart had almost stopped when he'd read the page. What was going on?

He felt small beads of moisture popped out across his forehead as he pulled on plastic gloves.

"Report," he snapped.

"BP 80 over 20. Unresponsive," a female voice stated.

Keep your cool. Think, man, think.

"Push meds."

He jerked off his stethoscope from around his neck, placed it on Jake's chest, and listened.

The beats sounded strong but slow.

"Epi—"

"BP rising," someone called from behind him.

"Eighty over fifty. Ninety-three over sixty-five and rising."

Rolling his shoulders, Scott released the tension knotted there, hard as a baseball. He turned to Jake's nurse. "Give another dose of Prograf. Check level in one hour. Blood gases every fifteen minutes till the hour and then every thirty minutes if stable. BP?"

"Low but steady."

"Okay, we're going to let him rest. Let his body adjust to the new heart. Stop any possibility of rejection. Watch him carefully. Page me if I'm needed."

Scott's hands shook. He'd almost lost control. Now he had to tell Hannah that Jake still wasn't out of danger.

Andrea placed a hand on his arm and said in a low voice, "Hannah's in the hallway. She's almost hysterical."

Scott took a deep breath and let it out slowly. He must get his rattled nerves under control before he saw Hannah. He pushed through the unit doors.

Hannah leaned against the wall, her face drained of color. She looked like she'd slide down the wall any second. When he opened his arms she stepped into them. A tremble went through her as she clung to him. He tightened his embrace.

"Scott, what's happening?"

He ran a hand down her hair, smoothing it,

allowing himself time to form the words he resisted saying.

"Jake is in rejection."

"Oh, my God, no."

Her tears dampened his shirt where her face was pressed to his chest.

"We've seen this before. But it'll be touch and go for a while. We may even have to relist him if the rejection can't be controlled. He'll have to be watched closely through the rest of the night. All we can do now is to wait and see if Jake's body will accept the heart."

Hannah pulled away and looked up at him. Terror, desolation and weariness filled her eyes. "Can I see him?"

"Yes, but only briefly."

Hannah noticed Scott's usual reassurance and confidence was missing. He wasn't telling her everything would be all right. A sick feeling hit her again. Scott was worried.

It was difficult to believe Jake had gotten his new heart and now it might kill him. She wanted to curl into a ball and hide, but she wouldn't. She had to remain strong, see Jake over this hurdle.

With effort Hannah prepared for what Jake would look like. She'd been warned he'd be swollen from being on the heart-lung machine. Tubes, a lot more than before, would be inserted into his body. It hurt to think of her small boy having to endure pain.

After washing her hands, she shakingly pulled on a gown and gloves. One of the nurses helped her with a mask. She found Jake behind glass doors, which were closed to form an isolation room.

The steady whoosh and puff of the respirator was ever-present. He was surrounded by beeping pumps and three of the staff. Hannah tuned all of it out. Taking slow, steady steps, she approached the bed. The light touch of Scott's hand at her back steadied her. He was her rock in the face of this ugly reality. She was thankful to have him there.

Jake wasn't as puffy as she'd feared. That was one positive. "He looks so pink," Hannah whispered. She hadn't seen such a healthy color on Jake's cheeks in a long time. The difference was remarkable. The dusky blue around his lips had disappeared. He looked beautiful. If only his body would embrace this heart.

The incision site made her flinch. Taking his

small limp hand in her gloved one, she'd make do with meager contact until she could hold him.

Hannah looked at Scott and whispered, "This heart has to work." She refused to believe otherwise.

Scott's hand flexed against her back.

To Jake she whispered, "I love you, honey." She watched for any indication he'd heard her. "Hang in there."

"Tomorrow we'll know more," Scott said from behind her. "We'll let him rest, give him a chance to adjust to the heart. If he improves we can start weaning him off the respirator. But the next twelve to twenty-four hours are crucial. You'll want to stay close."

Hannah slumped against him as tears ran down her cheeks.

Apparently Scott no longer cared what the staff thought or what the grapevine would say in the morning. His arm supported her as they walked out of the CICU.

Hannah had asked Scott a couple of times during the wee hours of the morning if she could come into the unit. He allowed it once but the next time he had to say no. Jake's blood pressure had plummeted again. Scott feared they were losing him, but Jake came through the episode and started doing much better. It looked like the adjustment period was over.

He'd wanted to sit with Hannah and give her some much-needed support but Jake required his attention. He couldn't remember a time when he'd felt so torn. Scott managed to go to the waiting area and check on Hannah around six in the morning. The lights were still off, and he found her staring into space in the dark room. The TV was in snow mode.

He flipped the switch, doing away with the electric storm, and gathered her to him. She laid her head on his chest and a soft sigh slipped through her lips. They said nothing for a long time. He struggled with having to leave her all alone when it was time to return to the unit.

At midmorning Scott returned to the waiting room to find Hannah asleep sitting up. His heart went out to her. It was pouring with rain outside, and despite the weak light Scott could see the exhaustion on her face. The weariness had to be both emotional and physical. A person could only take so much, and she'd had more than her share.

Scott hated to wake her but she needed to be in a bed. Outside the hospital rest area. He gave her a gentle shake.

Hannah's head jerked up. "What?" A wild look filled her eyes. She rose quickly. "Is Jake okay?"

"He's fine, honey. Doing much better, actually. I thought you'd like to go back for a visit."

She blinked once, twice. Her hair was mussed and she looked adorable. He wanted to gather her into his arms, take her home and tuck her into his bed.

Unable to act on the impulse, he settled for taking her hand and walking beside her down the hall. "Jake needs to rest and stay quiet the rest of the day. If he's still improving by this evening, we'll start weaning him from the respirator."

After gowning up to visit, Scott followed Hannah to Jake's bed. "I've ordered he remain sedated to prevent pain and to let him rest. That'll put him in the best shape for when the respirator is removed. I've left orders for the meds to be decreased later this evening allowing him to wake up a little."

"Is he out of the woods?"

"I believe so, but I'll know more when I see him this evening."

"Thank God." Hannah leaned over, picked up Jake's unresponsive hand and brought it to her cheek.

Scott's chest constricted to see the love Hannah expressed. What did it feel like to be on the receiving end of that kind of devotion? His heart ached with longing for something that could never be. He needed to leave before he said something that might end up hurting her. "I need to check on another patient. I'll be a minute."

He went to the nursing station and glanced at his notes, not really seeing them. Inhaling deeply, he let the breath out slowly. His hands trembled slightly. Hannah and Jake made him wish he was a different kind of person.

The nurse seated beside him gave him a curious look. He managed a smile, hoping it looked more normal than his rattled nerves indicated. Taking another deep breath, he returned to Hannah. "It's time to go. You can come back later."

Her green eyes fixed on his. "May I kiss him?"

Scott couldn't say no. "Sure. Just be careful."

On her toes as far as she could stretch, Hannah leaned over the rail. The bed had been adjusted to a higher than normal position. She couldn't quite reach Jake's head.

Without hesitation, Scott circled her waist with his hands and lifted her. Hannah's lips touched Jake's forehead. Holding her a second longer, he lowered her. She glanced back at him, her eyes full of gratitude. His chest swelled.

A hand still at her waist, he said, "Let's go. You need to rest too. You're almost dead on your feet." He lowered his voice. "You're coming home with me."

She gave him a defiant look and said in a low whisper, "No, I'm staying here."

He grinned. She hadn't disappointed him. Even worn out, she could put up a fight. "No, you're not, and that's the way it's going to be." His tone left no doubt he meant it. "Think about it. If anything were to happen to Jake I'm the first person who'd be called, which means you'd know right away." With complete confidence he knew his statement would put a stop to any argument she might make.

They made their way to the parking deck in silence. As the elevator doors closed, he slipped an arm around her waist and gathered her close, tucking her against him. She accepted his support. He liked having Hannah next to him. She fit.

As they exited the elevator and walked to the car, Hannah made no effort to leave his embrace. He helped her into his car, and she rested her head against the seat. Exhaling a sigh of exhaustion, she closed her eyes and immediately fell asleep. Scott adjusted her head so it rested on his shoulder.

Scott and Hannah stood in his living room, watching each other. Indecision hung in the air as if they were two magnets pulled together while at the same time being pushed apart. His gaze lingered on Hannah's brown hair then traveled over the curve of her cheek, paused at her breasts before following the length of her jeans-covered legs.

He wanted her in his bed, but she'd get no rest there. It wouldn't be fair to her. A physical relationship would imply there could be something more between them. That wasn't going to happen. He would leave her. He had to.

His eyes returned to hers. Those expressive green orbs had gone wide. The tell-tale rapid pulse in her neck caught his attention. Hannah recognized his desire. He had to send her to her bed before he tumbled her into his. "Get some sleep, Hannah."

She said nothing, turned and walked down the hall.

Scott decided he needed a shower. An ice-cold one.

Needing rest after a long night, he'd installed the one thing that could keep him awake right next door to his bedroom. What had he been thinking?

On the way to his room, Scott hesitated at her closed door. He brought his fist up to knock, but dropped his hand to his side. It would be disastrous if she opened the door. He would lose control. His body ached to have her. All the tension, emotion and adrenalin of the last twenty-four hours would find release. With a force of will he hadn't known he possessed, Scott moved on down the hall. The firm click of the door closing behind him echoed in his too-empty bedroom.

Scott was stepping out of the bathroom a few minutes later when the door to his room opened. Hannah stood partially in the entrance, as if she wasn't sure she'd be welcome. She wore the same

T-shirt she'd had on the other night. One sleek leg came into view. He wanted more.

His heartbeat rose, along with another part of his anatomy. He was grateful for the boxers he'd pulled on.

She didn't move. He waited. The next step had to be hers.

"I...uh...I don't want to be by myself." She made a movement towards him.

"Hannah, I can't just hold you."

"I know." The words were said so softly he almost didn't hear them. "I want to forget all the ugliness. To start living life again. To feel. I want you to make the loneliness go away for a little while." Scott enveloped her in a hug. Hannah wrapped her arms around his trim waist and pulled his warmth and strength closer. She wanted to burrow into him, to push the loneliness away. A ripple of awareness went through her, and she released a soft moan of pleasure. It felt wonderful, even right, to be in Scott's bedroom.

His look intensified. Drawing her snugly against the breadth of his chest, his lips came down on hers in a crushing kiss. Those same lips had brought her pleasure on many levels, smiling at her, reassuring her, making her laugh. A ripple of excitement raced through her body. She'd found her protective harbor.

Scott eased his hold, but his body remained tense, as if he was restraining his desire with effort. His kisses became a succession of gentle nibbles against her mouth. She leaned into him, asking for more, demanding it. Her hands slid up his arms to circle his neck, offering herself to him completely.

The sound of a man released from his pain surfaced from deep within Scott. He became the aggressor again. Giving her a couple of long caressing kisses, he then probed her mouth with a gentle flick of his tongue. She opened to him, surrendering. His tongue explored her mouth, conquering.

He lifted her, his hands cupping her behind. She tightened her arms about his neck.

A sound trickled out of her, a cross between a mewl and a hum.

She trusted him. Scott would take care of her.

Scott groaned in delight at the discovery Hannah wasn't wearing panties. He feared his need might pour over the dam wall of his control. Hannah had surprises. Sweet surprises.

His finger traced the place where a band of lace

should've been circling her thigh, before his hand traveled over the curve of her hip. Hannah pulled away and searched his face for a suspended moment before bringing her mouth to his again. Her kiss became damp, dense and daring as she caressed his lips with her own, as her tongue searched and found his.

She fed his raging need. He surrendered with a growl of unadulterated male desire.

Hannah giggled. She had to know exactly what kind of effect she was having on him.

His mouth feasted upon hers. Their tongues dueled. The hot, forceful motion of her tongue tasting and exploring his mouth tantalized him, testing his control. His manhood stood ridged between them. He would have Hannah, and there was no going back.

"Hannah…" Scott drawled in a strangled voice when she dragged her mouth from his. "You're so hot." He reached for her again, pulling her along the evidence of what she did to him. In a raspy whisper he said, "You do the sweetest things to me."

"You're kind of wonderful yourself." Her look was shy, sending a completely different message from the suggestive shift she made against him.

Her bashfulness ebbed and flowed. It was one of many facets of her personality Scott found intriguing. A lioness when fighting for her son, yet in a heated moment of passion she could still act and look like a lady. Someone he wanted to care for, protect. Scott found the combination of strength and timidity intriguing.

He studied her earnestly.

"What's wrong? Am I hurting you?" she asked, stirring as if she'd leave his arms.

He held her in place with a firm clasp of his hands under her amazing behind. Oh, yeah, she was hurting him, but in a good way. "Stay. I like you here. I want to look at you."

Hannah lowered her eyes then brought her gaze back to meet his.

"I want you in my bed." His words were little more than a husky sigh.

Her cool lips touched the fevered skin of his chest in acceptance, before moving her attention to his lips.

With her secure in his arms, Scott walked her backwards to the bed. Her lips remained tightly pressed against his as she followed his lead. Half seated, half lying, he brought her down with him. She shifted, gaining a more intimate position against him, pushing his ache higher. Searching her eyes, Scott found trust and openness and wanting there.

He needed to have her crave him as much as he did her. Something he'd never experienced before.

Scott found he was experiencing numerous firsts where she was concerned.

Hannah broke the heated kiss and smiled down at Scott. His lips curved into one of the sexy grins she loved so much. "Hannah…" The word drifted across her cheek like a sea breeze. Blood zipped through her veins. With a tender slip of his hand along her neck he guided her mouth down to meet his. She saw the reverence in his eyes before her lids lowered. The pure, perfect pleasure of his mouth against hers again made her heart soar.

His index finger crawled cross her thigh to the edge of her shirt, and slipped under. His hand gained her complete attention as it slid further up over her hip and across her back to settle at the curve of her breast. His fingertips danced away, leaving behind a straining ache to be touched.

She shuddered. The hunger throbbed low in her belly as primal as a native drum. Her hips lifted towards him, then pulled away and lifted again, before he brought her on top of him. The hard length of his desire pulsated against her belly. Their tongues touched, darted away, and came together to meet again.

Hannah's fingers wandered across his chest. Warm and solid, her hand hovered over the fine mat of hair there. Scott shifted beneath her as she continued her exploration. His heartbeat thumped steady and strong under her palm. Ignoring his murmur of protest, she lifted her mouth from his and placed a kiss above his heart.

His chest stilled, his breathing faltered.

With a rumble of pure manly pleasure coming from deep within him, Scott flipped her. He pushed the shirt she wore up and off, exposing her breasts.

He placed a tender, reverent kiss on the soft curve of one of the exposed mounds before his mouth moved to hover over the tip of the other breast. Hannah inhaled and her nipple brushed his partially open mouth.

With the tip of his tongue, Scott flicked the nipple straining to reach him. A shiver moved through her. Her eyes widened. Was the hunger she felt reflected in them?

"Please," Hannah begged, as she pushed at his boxers.

Scott stood, letting his underwear fall to the floor. He reached into his bedside-table drawer, found what he needed and sheathed himself. He rejoined her, taking her mouth in a long and lingering kiss. Moving between her legs, he entered her slowly. Reverently.

Hannah welcomed him into her heat, basking in it. Wrapping her legs around him, she pulled him to her. She joined him in the special dance of life as they found a rhythm that was theirs alone.

She tensed, gripped his shoulders and voiced her pleasure before a rumble of satisfaction began deep in his throat and built like thunder rolling into the night to boom as he joined her in paradise.

A feeling of power swept over Hannah as she lay cradled in Scott's arms. She'd made the always-in-control doctor lose it. The knowledge fueled her desire.

She'd never been the aggressor in lovemaking but with Scott it had been different. It amazed her. The freedom he allowed her to be herself endeared him to her even more. The curtain surrounding her heart and concealing her feelings fluttered open after years of stillness.

She was in love. Mountain high, valley low and river wide, in love.

Scott pushed her hair away from her forehead and kissed her.

"That was wonderful," Hannah said against his chest.

"The kiss or…?"

"Fishing for a compliment?"

"No, actions speak louder than words."

Hannah nipped his skin with her teeth.

"Watch it. That might lead to retaliation."

She giggled. "I wouldn't mind."

His hand skimmed over her hip. "I wouldn't either."

Neither said anything for a few minutes.

Was this the time and the place to ask? She had to know. She'd wondered for years. If she asked it might ruin everything but if she didn't she might never know. She needed to understand why.

Hannah brushed her hand back and forth over the mat of hair on his chest. "Scott, can I ask you something?"

"Sure." The word came out slowly, as if he was drifting off to sleep.

"Why?" With her cheek resting against his warm skin, she felt the catch in his breathing.

"Why what?" His voice no longer sounded drowsy.

"Why wouldn't you talk to me after that night?"

He stilled. His hand no longer caressed her side. "Because it couldn't go anywhere," he said quietly. "I would've only hurt you more. It should never have happened."

Hannah twisted around so she could look at him. "You think I didn't know that? I'd watched you with all the other nurses. But I did think our friendship deserved more credit than you gave it."

He didn't say anything for a long moment. "You're right. You were a stronger person than I gave you credit for being."

"Self-esteem get in the way, did it?" The question had a bitterness to it she'd not intended.

"I'll admit I was a little more than confident about my success with women, as you know."

She smiled. "A little?"

"Well, if it's any consolation I'm not as confident as I used to be." He shifted, moving away from her slightly. "As for the way I acted, for the first time in my life I found something I wanted as badly as I wanted to be a surgeon—you. I had no idea you were a virgin. I couldn't believe you chose to give that gift to me. I knew you were the type of woman who needed a forever kind of guy. I wasn't prepared to be the guy. The truth is you scared me."

She swallowed hard. There was nothing to lose by asking, "And now? Do I scare you?"

"No, now I'm scared *for* you."

"Why?" she asked softly, fear prickling her heart. Something told her she wouldn't like his answer.

"Do you remember me telling you my father is a doctor?"

She nodded.

"He's a wonderful guy, and a great doctor who loves people. He still makes house calls. But my father has a problem. He can't say no. It made my mother miserable and in turn it made him miserable. When I decided to go to medical school my mother cried. Not with joy but in disappointment. She said I'd be just like my dad. Married to my job."

Hannah wanted to yell that Scott was different. He already proved it in so many ways. Their relationship had nothing to do with his parents' marriage. Scott needed to give them a chance.

There must be another reason he wouldn't let her get close.

"That's not all there is to it, is it? Because all kinds of people have high-pressure careers and solid relationships."

"No, that isn't all. My parents divorced during my surgical fellowship. If anything, Mother got worse. She became more demanding, more in need of attention, but now it was from me and my brothers. Mother called us all the time, wanting this or that. During one period the calls numbered as many as ten or fifteen a day. My brothers have families so I tried to run interference and asked Mom to come and visit me for a few weeks. While she was staying with me she had an emotional breakdown and took an overdose of pills."

"Oh, Scott. I'm so sorry." She squeezed his hand. "Is she all right?" she asked quietly.

"She's fine now. Doing well. For the first time in a long time I really think she is starting to be happy."

He continued, as if he needed to talk.

"I had no idea she'd become so depressed. I should've known but I was so involved in my work I couldn't see it." He looked down at their clasped hands. "She called me, and I didn't go, didn't even answer her call. She'd gotten to where she was calling me almost hourly, day in, day out. Sometimes I answered, other times I didn't. I didn't want to encourage her.

"That day was no different. It had been a crazy day, with one patient going into cardiac arrest, two more being admitted. My voice mail was full of messages begging me to come home, but I still had afternoon rounds to make.

"I arrived home to find her passed out on her bed in her best dress with a pill bottle in her hand."

"And you've been blaming yourself ever since."

"Yeah." The word was said so softly she almost didn't hear it.

She cupped his face. "It wasn't your fault."

"It's easy to say, but I don't think I'll ever really believe it. The overdose was bad enough but Mom said she wanted nothing more to do with me."

"That can't be true!"

"Well, it was at the time. Now we do have some semblance of a relationship but we're just going through the motions. Both of us are dancing around the elephant in the room when we see each other."

"Have you sat down and really had a heart to heart with your mom?"

"No, I just want to forget and move on."

"I don't think you ever will until you two kick the elephant out the door."

He squeezed her to him. "You might be right." He hesitated. "It also hit home that horrible day that I was no different from my father. I knew then I had no business having a wife and family. I'm incapable of setting boundaries for myself. I'm too wrapped up in my work. My job will always come first."

Hannah wrapped her arms around him and gave him a hug. She said nothing for a long moment. She couldn't let him know how she felt. He was already starting to run. She was done being the goodbye girl. Maybe with more time she could convince him he was wrong about himself, that his mother had been speaking out of her own pain. For now she had to tell him what he needed to hear. "I don't expect any more than your friendship."

The tension in Scott's body eased.

CHAPTER EIGHT

No light beamed through the bedroom window when Hannah woke up.

Jake. How's Jake?

She reached for her cell phone on the bedside table. The space beside her was still warm. Scott hadn't been gone long.

Battery dead.

Flinging the spread off, she looked for a phone. Finding none, she pulled on the first thing she saw. It was one of Scott's T-shirts. Her bare feet made a padding noise as she went to the door and pulled it open. A gurgle came from down the hall. Coffee-pot. Kitchen. There'd be a phone there. Her throat tightened as she hurried toward the sound. Panic welled. She had to check on Jake.

She stopped short at the sight of Scott at the kitchen table. He held a newspaper, a cup of coffee within his reach.

He glanced at her. "Evening," he drawled.

"I've got to call the hospital." She frantically searched the kitchen for a phone.

"Settle down. Jake's fine. I checked in. They're already starting to wean him from the respirator."

The calmness in his voice annoyed her, but her heart slowed its pace. "Really?"

"Yes. Really." He gave her a lazy smile.

Relief washed over her.

"I'm his doctor, remember?" Scott grabbed her arm and pulled her into his lap. His lips found hers. They'd slept and loved the afternoon away without Scott's beeper sounding an alarm. Even after the time they'd shared in bed, Hannah still hungered for him. He'd left her in bed again but based on his actions earlier in the day and again later in the afternoon she knew he wouldn't go far. Scott had been a wonderfully attentive lover.

She couldn't resist returning his kiss but she had to put a stop to this before she went past the point of no return. The truth was, though, that had already happened.

She pushed away and stood, moving out of his reach. "Uh, about last night, I mean today, I—"

"You needed someone and I was there. Being a friend. How about a cup of coffee or tea before we go to the hospital? Would you like something to eat now or wait until we get back?"

Scott certainly wasn't placing any importance on what had occurred between them. His calm demeanor almost made her smack him. Those had been the most amazing moments of her life and Scott was treating them as if they had been no big deal. If he could act cool about their lovemaking then so could she.

Resting back in his chair, with a slight grin on his lips, he acted as if it was a normal everyday occurrence to have her in his home. Despite the lack of sleep during the night and today, he appeared well rested. He'd already dressed. His royal blue polo shirt and khaki pants made him look like he was ready for a round of golf.

Heavens, she was wearing one of his thin white shirts. Her eyes dropped to what she wore. His shirt barely reached the top of her thighs. Heat rushed up her neck and settled in her cheeks. She crossed her arms over her breasts. Scott had seen much more, touched every inch of her, but she wasn't used to parading around half-dressed in front of a man.

"Why didn't you say something?" she squeaked. "I'm going to get dressed."

He raised an eyebrow and made a low chuckle. "Are you kidding? I was enjoying the sight of you in my T-shirt, in my kitchen."

She whirled to leave.

Scott pushed back his chair, stood and caught her arm. "I'll get you something to cover up with. Fix yourself a cup of tea. Settle for a minute." He left.

Going to the pot, Hannah found a teabag and poured water into a cup. After the stress of the last couple of days, and especially yesterday, on many levels, she needed to soothe her nerves. She was still standing by the counter when Scott returned.

He handed her a robe. Scrambling into it, she found it fell below her knees, giving her some sense of security. She pulled the belt tight. The tangy smell of Scott permeated the robe.

"Better?" he asked.

"Much, thanks."

Scott returned to his seat and picked up his coffee mug, still grinning. It was clear he was enjoying her discomfort.

Pushing against the leg of a chair, he scooted it out. "Come and sit next to me."

Hannah approached the chair with trepidation.

The whole scene smacked too much of marital bliss. It made her wish for things Scott had said could never be.

She sank into the chair. "Why're we taking our time getting to the hospital? Don't you need to check on Jake? I need to see him."

"You didn't get much uninterrupted rest. I was giving you as much time as possible to sleep. Instead of doing that, you came storming through the door." His lips turned up at the corners.

Hannah flushed all over. Yes, he had kept her busy as if he'd held himself in check for all the years they'd been apart. "Please don't make fun of me. My first thought was of Jake. He's all I've got."

Scott's face sobered and the skin along his jaw tightened. He acted as if he was going to say something, before his face eased and he returned to his easygoing manner. "When you finish your tea, we'll go."

"I need to get a quick shower."

His eyes turned dark and his voice dipped low. "Would you like some company?"

Heat coiled within her. For a second Hannah was tempted to say yes. "No, I think I can manage by myself." She hurried out of the room, fearing she might change her mind.

Scott groaned.

How much could a healthy male take? Waking with Hannah's warm body nestled close and having her come into his kitchen with the scent of him lingering on her was one of the most erotic things he'd ever experienced. He longed for it all. Hannah, the job, a family. Could he have that ideal life?

She'd said Jake was all she had. He'd wanted to argue the point. Tell her she had him too. But could he honestly make that promise? Pulling out his cell phone, Scott checked on Jake and another patient in the hope Hannah would be dressed by the time he'd finished. He needed to get his mind on something else. If he didn't find a way to keep busy, he might do something stupid, like stepping into the shower with her. Or telling Hannah he loved her.

Would she welcome him with open arms?

Scott groaned. There were other problems. Jake's recovery concerned him more than he'd let on to Hannah. There was always a chance Jake could have difficulty getting off the respirator because he had been on it before going into surgery. Scott hoped and prayed removal went smoothly for everyone's sake.

"Ready?" Hannah had entered the living room without him noticing. A quizzical look crossed her face. "You're deep in thought."

There was a fresh, wholesome smell to her. Perfect. She wore a simple light green shirt and a short blue denim skirt that showed off her incredible legs. Scott resisted the urge to pull her to him and kiss her past all reason. If he did that, they'd never make it to the hospital any time soon.

She stepped closer. "Everything okay with Jake?"

Her question brought him back to reality. He had to leave. He'd never run away from a woman before, but he felt the need to put some space between himself and Hannah. "How about we see for ourselves?"

Scott pulled into the hospital parking lot a few minutes after seven. Hannah had to wait until after shift change before she could see Jake. Scott regretted he couldn't let her come back with him, but shift change was the one time of day the nurses' word was law.

When most of the patients' reports had been given, Scott asked Jake's nurse to call the waiting room and tell Hannah she could come through.

His lips curved upward as he watched Hannah hurry to Jake's bed. Her smile made him feel like the greatest man on earth. A superhero. His skill as a surgeon had helped to put a joyful look on her face. With that knowledge came immense satisfaction.

Scott moved to stand beside her. "Jake's making great progress so far. We'll be going down five breaths at a time over the next few hours and then try to remove the tube first thing in the morning.

"Nurse, I want a blood gas drawn every fifteen minutes. Cut back on the dopamine and Captopril." He made a notation on Jake's chart.

"He looks better than he did yesterday. Even his incision area doesn't look as awful." Hannah ran a caressing finger along Jake's arm.

Hannah showed her caring through touch. Scott especially enjoyed it when he was on the receiving end of emotion. The stroke of her hand had a way of making him feel as if he was the best man in the world for her. It was already killing him to think about having to let her go.

"During the night we will work toward removing the respirator. The longer we wait the harder it is to remove. Because Jake was on the respirator before surgery it's even more important he comes off it soon," Scott said. "You'll be surprised at how fast things will improve afterwards. We'll continue to keeping a close watch on him."

"Jake certainly doesn't need any additional problems."

"I don't want him to have any more problems either. He's a special little guy. I'm doing everything I know to see it doesn't happen. I think he's past the worst." Scott gave her shoulder a quick squeeze. Something as simple as giving Hannah a reassuring touch sent heat hissing through him.

She continued to look at her amazing little miracle.

"Do you think you could eat now?" Scott asked.

"Yeah. I'm starving, but I hate to leave him."

"His nurse knows we're but a phone call away. Hunger's a good sign your nerves are settling down."

His certainly weren't. A different kind of hunger gnawed at him.

After picking up a drive-through meal, they returned to Scott's place. With their dinner completed, Scott gave Hannah one of his piercing looks that said in no uncertain terms he wanted her. He scooped her up and carried her to his bed. This time their lovemaking was slow and sweet. Afterwards Hannah curled into him and settled into a peaceful, deep sleep, enhanced by dreams of what could be.

The next morning Scott left her with a swift, but fervent kiss before they parted in the stairway. With Jake improving and a kiss from Scott on her lips, Hannah's heart felt lighter than it had in years.

She'd barely been in CICU a few minutes when Jake's nurse asked her to leave. It was time for the respiratory therapist to remove the respirator.

Hannah sat, paced and sat again. Would Jake be able to come off? Would he stay off? What if he had to be put back on?

Stop.

She had to quit thinking. Thinking led to an all-consuming fear. Despite her efforts not to look at the clock, she watched each slow minute pass. With any luck this would be the last time she'd have to endure this type of wait.

The desk phone rang. Hannah stared at the pink-coated volunteer who answered it. She looked at Hannah. "The nurse says you can come back now."

The tube was gone from Jake's mouth. He lay at a slight angle, propped on pillows with an oxygen canula under his nose. A weak smile came to his lips as Hannah approached. Her heart swelled. It felt like years since she'd seen his lips curl upwards.

"Hello, honey." She beamed to the point that her cheeks ached. The bed had been lowered and she leaned across Jake, placing her cheek against his.

The nurse still had his hands secured. Hannah put her index finger in his palm and he wrapped his fingers around hers. His breathing remained labored, but not enough for her to be too concerned. He was breathing on his own. That was what mattered. Catching the corner of her shirt, she wiped the moisture away from her eyes. "I love you."

"M-o-m-m-y." He mouthed the word but she heard no sound.

"Do you have anything to put on his lips? They're so dry and cracked," Hannah asked.

The nurse handed her lip balm. Hannah applied it, welcoming the opportunity to have even such a small part in his care.

Jake's eyes focused on Hannah for a second before his eyelids drooped. The sparkle of his childhood had yet to return but it would soon. She said a prayer of thanks for Scott's surgical skills and for the family who had given her child life again. The knowledge of what the family of the donor was suffering troubled Hannah, but she was grateful for the gift of Jake's life. She would make sure their gift was honored by taking excellent care of Jake.

The nurse allowed Hannah to remain at his bedside most of the day. The time passed in a blur of activity, which was a relief from the mind-numbing worry and boredom of the past few days. Hannah hadn't seen Scott since earlier that morning, but knew he had to be in surgery. She missed him. He'd come to see them when he could, she had no doubt.

By the middle of the afternoon only one nurse was required for Jake's care. The central line had been removed, along with the catheter. The machines monitoring vitals, two chest tubes and a pacemaker were all that remained.

Scott finally made it by to see them in the early evening. The nurse smiled knowingly at Hannah and Scott then left them alone.

"Doesn't he look wonderful?" Hannah asked, unable to contain her happiness.

"He does." Scott's smile reached his eyes. "He's doing great. If tomorrow goes as well as today, he'll be going to the floor."

"Wonderful. I can stay with him all the time then."

"I'll miss having you next to me when that happens, but it's nice to see you happy." Scott's look turned solemn. "I wanted us to have dinner tonight, but I've got emergency surgery. Please don't stay too late. I don't like you being in the parking deck by yourself." His finger traced the line of her jaw. "Go to my house. Get some rest," he whispered, and slipped her keys.

Her heart contracted. She felt cherished, as if she had someone to stand beside her. It was wonderful to no longer be alone. Not having experienced those feelings for a long time, she wrapped the sensation around her and basked in its warmth. "I won't. I'll go after I see Jake, I promise."

Scott nodded, his gaze never leaving hers.

Hannah glanced around, then lowered her voice. "I appreciate you taking care of both my son and me. You've been a great friend. I'm glad you were here when we needed you." She gave him a bright smile.

"My pleasure."

In response to his husky tone, a sizzle of delight zipped through her.

In the same sensual timbre, he said, "I wish I could kiss you…" he glanced around "…but…"

She reached for his hand, catching his little finger for a moment then releasing it. "I do too."

He looked into her eyes for an extended moment filled with wishing, regret, and a promise before he left. The warmth that had surrounded her went with him. Hannah understood why he hadn't kissed her but that didn't keep her from being disappointed.

Much later Scott slipped into bed beside her. She scooted next to him. The contentment she'd been missing had returned, engulfing her.

"Shh…go back to sleep," Scott said softly in her ear as his arms drew her back against him.

"Jake?"

"He's fine, honey. Sleeping when I left."

She glanced at the clock. One a.m.

"Are you okay?" The blood hummed through her veins, being so close to him. The roughness of his beard brushed across her cheek.

"Yeah, tired. Sorry to wake you."

"A doctor's life isn't always their own. Coming home at all hours is part of my life. I understand."

"A lot of women wouldn't see it that way."

"Well, I'm not just any woman. I know firsthand what you do is important." His arms tightened around her for a second then eased. Goose-bumps popped up along her arms.

He placed a quick kiss behind her ear. "Thank you."

The words were thick with emotion, as if she'd given him a precious gift.

"Okay, we're off." Hannah made a buzzing noise like an airplane as she circled the white plastic spoon in a flying motion toward Jake's mouth.

He giggled. Like a baby bird waiting for a worm, he opened his mouth. Hannah dipped the spoon into his mouth. Scott stood at the door, watching mother and child totally absorbed in each other. His chest swelled with pride. This was his reward for the years of medical school and lost sleep of his intern years. If only he could keep Hannah as happy for the rest of her life. He shook his head. He had no business contemplating such things. They were never to be.

Scott winced at the memories of his family meals. There had been a few nice ones early in his life, but as his parents' marriage had disintegrated during his teenage years, few if any had been peaceful. It was hard to remember the warmth that he felt in this small hospital room at any meal.

Hannah might understand now what his job entailed, but after a while his dedication to his profession would grow stale, start to divide them. He didn't want what had happened between his parents to happen to him and Hannah. That would be a pain he couldn't bear.

He ached to be on the inside of the love he was witnessing, instead of standing on the outskirts. Could he manage having a family and a growing transplant program at the same time?

What if he set boundaries? Learned to say no? Accepted help? Could he make his professional life different than his father's?

No. He wouldn't take the chance. He loved Hannah and Jake enough to protect them from him.

Scott left without disturbing them.

* * *

By the end of the day most of the tubes and lines attached to Jake had been removed. The two large chest tubes used to drain fluid and the pacemaker wires were all that remained. They would be taken out after he went to the floor.

Hannah disliked Jake's hands having to remain tied. She *ached* to hold him. She'd have to settle for small hugs for a while longer. They weren't as satisfying as having him sit in her lap, secure against her chest, but that would come.

She'd thought Scott would've been by to see them before now. At least visit between surgeries.

Life would be busy during the next year. There would be little time to devote to a relationship, even if Scott wanted one—and he gave no indication of wanting that. She wasn't fooling herself into believing he gave any thought to a future with her. She wished she could get Scott to see they could be a family if he would open his mind to the possibility of a relationship. But it was more than she could hope for.

This thing between them had simply been a convenient interlude.

She had to stop driving herself crazy with what-ifs. One question still wouldn't go away. How had she let Scott become such an important and necessary part of her life so quickly?

"They're ready for Jake on the step-down unit," his nurse said, interrupting Hannah's musings.

Jake was sitting up in the middle of his bed with a smile on his face. His nurse had already loaded his belongs onto the far end of the bed.

"Ready to go, sweetheart?" Hannah asked him.

"Go, brrmm, brrmm," he said, driving his pretend car.

It was hard to believe how quickly he was recovering. Almost hourly he gathered more strength. His personality was returning too.

Hannah laughed. "Yes, brrmm, brrmm."

With Hannah's help, the nurse maneuvered the bed down the hall and into the elevator. It felt so good to be doing something active after so many hours of waiting and worrying. They pushed Jake's bed into a wing of the hospital Hannah had never seen.

The charge nurse met them in the hall. "We're glad Jake's doing so well. We've been looking forward to meeting you."

Hannah didn't understand the comment. Why would the nurses be interested in her? Had the grapevine been talking about her and Scott?

The nurse settled Jake into his room and checked his IVs. Hannah watched as the telemetry to monitor Jake's heart rate in the nurses' station was attached. His nurse also hooked him up to a blood-pressure and a pulse-ox machine.

Hannah scrutinized everything. Being a nurse was an innate part of her. She may not be nursing at present but she'd not forgotten the safety precautions.

"You'll need to continue to wear a gown and gloves," his nurse said.

"Even when I sleep?"

"You can go without covering if you sleep on the other side of the room. And there can be no visitors outside immediate family."

"That won't be a problem. There's just me." Those words sounded sad to even Hannah's own ears.

When Jake slipped into a peaceful sleep, Hannah went down the hall to buy a canned drink. On her way back she passed a partially open door to a patient's room. The respiration and heart monitor were buzzing. No parent was staying with the child. She'd mentioned the patient to Jake's nurse earlier, saying how difficult it must be for the parents not to stay with their child. Hannah was grateful she wasn't in the same situation.

Searching the hallway, she saw no staff members headed her direction. She looked into the room. A child of about two years old was lying on his back unmoving and turning a dusky blue.

Hannah pushed the door open as a man from housekeeping came around the corner.

"Get some help. Stat!" She didn't wait to see if he did as ordered. She plopped her drink on the table on her way to the bedside. Reaching the child, she pushed the nurses' call button. No answer.

She placed her hand on the child's chest. There was no rise or fall. Quickly lowering the bed rail, Hannah rolled the boy on his side. She placed her cheek near his mouth. No breath.

The beeping of the monitor still pierced the air, but she tuned it out. This child would die if she didn't do something. Had he aspirated into his lungs? She checked the child's airway.

She had to start CPR.

Where were the nurses? Why wasn't someone coming?

The boy was turning bluer. She couldn't wait. Covering the child's mouth with hers and holding his nose closed, she blew enough air into his lung to raise the child's chest, then began compressions to the sternum.

Minutes crawled by. Still no one came. She continued working.

Where was everyone? Couldn't they hear the monitor? People as far away as Africa should be able to hear it.

She was going to have to use the defibrillator. Hadn't the crash cart been outside the door? It was her sole chance to save this child.

The housekeeping man stuck his head in the door and said help was on the way. There'd been a code blue at the other end of the hall.

"There's a code blue here," Hannah snapped between compressions.

The man stared at her.

"Two, there is, three, a cart, four, outside, five, the door, six, get it, seven, now."

The housekeeper didn't return pushing the crash cart. Instead Scott appeared.

"Hannah, I'll handle this. You push the meds. They're in the cart." He handed her a keyring with a key held between two fingers. "We'll worry about the legalities later."

She found the meds. Double, triple checking

the dosage on the code card against what was in her hand, she stepped to the other side of the bed. Pushing the needle into the portal of the IV, she said words of thanks that it had already been placed. She pressed the plunger down slowly.

"Step back," Scott commanded.

He placed the paddles of the defibrillator on the child's chest.

With the electric shock, the boy's chest rose then fell, then rose and fell again on its own.

"Get the oxygen mask on him. Two liters."

"Yes, sir." Hannah unwrapped the plastic tubing and turned on the oxygen at the head of the bed. Fitting the small plastic mask over the child's nose and mouth, she watched as Scott checked the boy's pulse. Scott pulled his stethoscope from around his neck and began listening to the boy's chest.

"We've got him back. Good work, Hannah."

A charge nurse rushed into the room, stopping short. "I just heard."

"He's stable. A CBS, panel, and gases need to be drawn. Let Dr. Carter know what happened. This is his patient. Also let the supervising nurse know I'd like to see her," Scott told the nurse in a stern voice.

He turned his attention to Hannah. "You did a fine bit of nursing here. This boy wouldn't have lived without you." He smiled across the bed at her as he reset the monitor and continued to check the numbers. "You can have a spot on my team any time."

She glowed under Scott's praise. He was right, they *had* worked well together. "Thanks. It was pretty scary there for a few minutes."

CHAPTER NINE

HANNAH glanced at her sleeping child when Scott opened the door enough to stick his head in. He'd been stopped by a staff member when they'd passed the nurses' station on their way back to Jake's room. Smiling, he backed out, returned with a mask in his hand then came inside and closed the door behind him.

The dark shadow along his jaw gave him a roguish look, a bad-boy appeal. She liked it. Her fingers itched to skim across his cheek while her heart raced at the sight of him. Hannah met Scott halfway across the room. A slow and sensual smile covered his lips. She had no doubt his thoughts were running similar to hers. They'd not really spent any time together in the last couple of days. She'd come to depend on him, accept him as part of her life. She'd missed him.

His smoldering eyes made her afraid she might flash-burn on the spot. Reaching for her, Scott took her hand and towed her toward the door. There they wouldn't immediately be seen by anyone entering the room or through the window to the hall. With his back against the wall and his feet spread apart, he pulled her close.

"I've missed you." His words rumbled as his lips skimmed over her check en route to her mouth as a finger pulled her mask down over her chin.

A tingle traveled along her spine. Hannah shivered as she molded her body to Scott's and brought her mouth to his. Scott took the invitation, grazing her lips, before he dipped to explore her more completely. The kiss pushed any thoughts away except for those hot and heavy with need that begged to be fulfilled. Scott's kiss communicated the same desperation.

A bolt of longing shot through Hannah. She gripped his waist. Molten heat pooled in the lower part of her body. With a sigh Hannah met his demands with those of her own. Her hands slid over the expanse of his chest to wrap around his neck. A fire blazed in her center. By the time Scott's lips had left hers, their breaths came in small gasps.

Hannah traced the nape of his neck with her

fingertips. His hand scanned her ribs, down her hip until it cupped her behind. Shifting, he fit her more snugly to him. The light, caressing kisses Scott was placing down one side of her neck made her knees buckle. Pressed against him, she didn't have to guess at his desire. It was evident. Hannah shifted her hips forward. He held her securely, a moan originating deep in his throat.

The prickle of his whiskers sent a shudder along her spine. They brushed her sensitive skin as his mouth found the hollow of her neck and he murmured, "You sure taste good."

Heat simmered then boiled in her as it flowed to her center. She wanted to hold onto this feeling for ever.

Hannah surrendered her neck and pushed closer. Scott's hand aided her movement forward. A yearning built in her like a summer electrical storm. He retraced his path with tiny nips of his teeth. His low rumble of satisfaction brought her a wave of delight. Going up on her toes, she silently asked for more.

Scott's tongue followed the shell of her ear. A tingle shot through her like water sizzling in oil. Her fingers dug into his back in an unspoken demand for more of everything.

"Mommy…" The soft call pierced the mist of sexual need. Hannah jerked away. Once again, Scott's hands had made her forget where she was. Scott groaned at the interruption.

"Bad timing?" Hannah giggled.

"You've no idea," Scott muttered. His body had some type of radar that zeroed in on Hannah's like a heat-seeking missile. The woman didn't have to be looking at him for his body to react.

"I think I might."

It was nice to know he wasn't the only one who forgot where they were when they were together. Hannah met his gaze and her hand cupped his cheek. Scott eased his hold but didn't let go of her. "I seem to lose control around you."

"Mommy…"

"Coming, honey."

What had he been thinking? Kissing his patient's mother in the little boy's room certainly showed poor professional conduct. That was just it, he didn't think around Hannah. He gazed down at her. Hannah's eyes were wide with expectation. Her sweet lips were plump and cherry colored. She had the look of a woman who'd been thoroughly kissed, and wanted more.

Oh, yeah. He'd like to do it again.

The need for her still throbbed within him.

He gave her a quick peck on the lips, then let her go. "I need to be a heart surgeon and check on my favorite patient." Pulling the mask out of his pocket, he fit it over his mouth before he approached Jake's bed.

"Hi, there, buddy," Scott said. "Remember me? I'm Dr. Mac." Scott pulled down his mask and gave Jake one of his Hollywood smiles before replacing the covering.

Scott picked up the disposable stereoscope hanging on the rail of the bed and listened to Jake's chest. "I need to give your new heart a listen for a sec."

"Mommy," Jake whispered. Hannah turned to pick up her mask before she stepped beside Scott.

"I'm right here. Be real still for Dr. Mac."

Jake watched his movements with interest. He was a bright little boy anyone would be glad to call his son. It wasn't a thought he should be having.

"His heart has a strong, steady beat. But I do want to pace it for a couple of days." Scott glanced at Hannah and saw the look of panic wash over her face. "Nothing's wrong. If I pace the heart it'll fall into a solid rhythm. The pacemaker gives the heart a little help so it doesn't have to work too hard."

She nodded.

"I see you still have Bear," Scott said to Jake as he touched the toy clipped to the bed. "We'll get those chest tubes out today so you can get out of bed and play some." To Hannah he said, "I'll write the orders before I go back to surgery."

"You're going back to the OR? You look like you need some rest."

"That bad, huh?" Scott chuckled. He appreciated the concern in her voice. It felt good to have Hannah fuss over him.

"I didn't say you look bad."

His grin grew. "So I look good?"

"Oh." She swatted his arm. "You know what I mean."

"I do. But I like seeing you flustered." Hannah returned his smile. Scott looked back to find Jake watching them. "I've got to go. They'll be waiting for me in surgery. Hannah?"

Her eyes lifted.

"Have dinner with me?"

"I…don't know. I need to be here with Jake."

"What if we make it a late meal? Jake will be

asleep. I'll order Chinese take-out and we can eat in the garden. We wouldn't be too far away."

She didn't answer right away.

Was Hannah trying to put some distance between them? He should be doing the same thing, instead of acting like the family man he could never be. But he couldn't back away yet. "Please. You don't have to stay any longer than you feel comfortable."

"Okay, but I want sweet and sour chicken, and fried rice."

He grinned. "You've got it. I'll see you around eight."

"Don't forget the fortune cookies."

He raised his thumb in the air and said goodbye to Jake before pulling the door closed behind him.

For Hannah the rest of the day was spent caring for Jake. The interruptions continued with doctors and nurses checking in. She and Jake did take a nap, but her peaceful sleep was sabotaged by thoughts of Scott. Where did she fit into his plans? Did she fit at all? Was this relationship going anywhere? She wanted him, but did he want her? Even with all the unknowns she still looked forward to seeing him again.

The thoracic surgery fellow came in to remove Jake's chest tubes. The nurse had warned Hannah it would be painful for Jake. The fellow asked Hannah if she wished to leave the room, but she declined the offer. She was a nurse. She'd be able to handle it. Besides, the fellow wasn't someone Jake knew. He'd be scared without her.

The fellow clipped the sutures holding the chest tubes in place then pulled them out with a steady motion. Jake's body tensed, tears streamed over his cheeks. His hands pulled against the restraints securing them.

Moisture welled in Hannah's eyes and fell. Never in her life had she wanted to scream "Stop!" louder or longer. Her hands gripped the metal rail until her knuckles turned white and her fingers blue. She knew this pain was necessary, but her mother's heart howled to have it done with.

"It'll be over soon, honey," Hannah said as calmly as she could in spite of the knot lodged in her throat.

As the fellow finished he told Hannah she could remove the restrains. Whimpering, Jake reached out to her. She lifted him into her arms, holding him tight as she cooed.

Exhausted, Jake soon quieted and fell asleep. Hannah settled into the wooden rocker, enjoying the feel of his small warm body against hers. Finally, she was able to hold her baby close.

When she finally put Jake down for the night he made a noise as if awakening. She patted his bottom until he settled again. Glancing at the clock, she saw she was running late and had to rush to change into tan slacks and a red cable sweater for her date with Scott.

The phone rang.

Her heart jumped. Was Scott calling to cancel?

The floor clerk was on the line, telling her Dr. McIntyre would be there soon. He was seeing a patient in CICU. Hannah's heart settled into a steady rhythm again, but her breathing remained faster than normal.

Twenty minutes later, Scott came to the door. "Sorry I'm late. I hate you always having to wait for me."

"I don't mind."

"You really don't, do you?"

"No. I know the importance of what you do. I'm just glad to see you."

Scott dressed in jeans and a striped button-down shirt reminded Hannah of how appealingly male he was. His shirt was tucked in, which emphasized his trim waist. His sleeves were rolled up over tan forearms. No man had ever looked better.

His smile reached his eyes. "It's nice to see you too. Our food's at the front desk. We'll pick it up on the way to the garden."

Hannah started in the direction of the elevator, but Scott took her hand and directed her into a stairway.

"Where're we going?"

"Down this way." He pinned her against the wall of the stairwell and his lips found hers. Long, lustful and luscious moments later he released her. "There's way too much interest in what I do around here. And I get a kick out of sneaking around, don't you?" He winked at her.

Hannah laughed and followed him down the stairs. Scott even made dinner at the hospital an adventure. She enjoyed seeing the kid come out in him. His job was a serious one. He needed a release from the life-and-death decisions that made up his world.

At the bottom of the stairs, Scott peeked out the

door and gave her a quick peck on the lips before they stepped through it. "Wait here," he said in a conspiratorial tone, before walking across the lobby. Scott spoke to a woman behind the welcome desk. She smiled and handed him two big bags. "Thanks, Helen. I owe you one."

Scott charmed young and the old. He'd gone one better with her, he'd made her fall in love with him. Hard. Could she convince him to make her and Jake a part of his life?

Looking both ways, as if he were a spy, Scott returned to her and took her hand again. Hannah snickered at his antics. His lips lifted into a sexy grin. Her breath caught. He led her to the drink machines, where they made their selections.

The garden looked lovely in the dusk of the summer day. A few late-blooming flowers gave off sweet scents. The setting sun shone brightly on one side, while the other side of the garden remained encased in shadow. They followed a curved walk around to the most secluded area. At a stone bench, Scott stopped.

"Wait before you sit." He poked through one of the bags, pulling out a camping lantern and a green and yellow plaid blanket. Flipping the blanket a couple of times, he settled it across the bench.

Hannah watched in fascination as he lit the lantern and placed it on the ground in front of the bench. Bowing like a maître d', Scott offered her a place on the bench.

Picking up the other bag, he handed her a white box from it. "Sweet and sour chicken, ma'am."

"Thank you, sir."

He dug further and came out with another container.

"What did you get?" She leaned over to peer into the container as he opened it.

"Nosy, aren't you?" he teased.

"I am. What're you having?"

"Mongolian beef."

"Ooh, that stuff's hot."

"Yes, like me," he quipped, making his brows rise and fall.

Hannah laughed. Something she did a lot when Scott was around. There had been little laughter in the last few years in her and Jake's life. It was nice to have it back, even for a short while.

"Here's your fried rice."

Hannah took it. "This is nice, thank you. I'm glad to get out of the room for a while." She picked at her chicken with her chopsticks. "I haven't been out here before. I'll have to bring Jake. No, I can't. He can't be around people for a few months."

"I wish I could tell you it was okay, but we can't take any chances he might catch something."

"I know. I'll bring him when we come for a visit. By the way, why didn't you tell me taking chest tubes out was so horrible?" She screwed up her face at the memory.

"It's rough. That's why I didn't do it myself. I don't want Jake to have that memory of me."

"Why not?"

"I want us to be friends and removing chest tubes isn't a friendly thing to do."

Her chest contracted to think it mattered to Scott whether or not Jake liked him.

As they ate, Hannah enjoyed the deep roll of Scott's voice. They discussed the movies they'd seen. She learned they both enjoyed Westerns and wished more were being made. Another thing they had in common. When they'd finished, Scott started gathering their empty containers. He pulled a couple of small packages out of another bag, like a magician performing a trick.

"Want your fortune cookie now?"

"I'd love it."

Opening his, he laughed.

"What?" she asked, leaning over until her shoulder rested against his. "Let me see." She took the small slip of paper from him. "What's so funny?" She handed it back.

"Haven't you ever heard about adding 'in bed' to the end of the fortune? 'Your talents will prove to be especially useful this week...in bed.'"

A flush covered her face. She couldn't meet his eyes. "It does give it a new meaning."

"Yeah, it does." The humor in his voice had disappeared, leaving it deep and raspy. She glanced at Scott from hooded eyes. His sea-blue gaze captured hers.

Hannah saw his desire. Hot, rich, deep. It pulled at her. But that was all it was, she had to remind herself, sexual desire. She couldn't let it drag her under. He'd made no promises. She wanted, no, needed more than a meeting of their bodies. Especially from Scott.

Scott leaned toward her as if planning to kiss her, but when a mother with a child in a stroller came around the curve in the walk, he straightened. Saying nothing, Scott began gathering the rest of the remains of their meal. Hannah helped.

When her hand brushed his, Scott captured it, turned it over and kissed the inside of her wrist. A tremor rolled through her. With everything packed away, he took her hand and they slowly walked back into the hospital.

Hannah didn't want the evening to end. Scott seemed to agree.

In the stairwell, before he opened the door to the floor, they shared a passionate meeting of lips that was much too short. With a final kiss to her cheek, Scott said, "I'll miss having you in my bed tonight."

Her stomach fluttered. "I'll miss being there, but you know I have to be here with Jake."

"I do and I'd expect nothing less from you. You're a wonderful mother."

"Thanks for understanding. I know what it is to be left and I'd never do it to Jake."

Darkness filled Scott's eyes.

"I didn't mean you."

A dry smile came to his lips. "I realize you could mean me."

Hannah cupped his cheek and smiled at him. "I could, but in this case I don't."

At Jake's room, Scott stopped long enough to review the med chart posted on the outside of the door. Dressed to enter, they stepped toward the sleeping child's bed.

Careful not to disturb Jake, Scott pulled off the sheet and checked the tube sites. "They look good."

"I'm proud of him. He's a trouper." Hannah tipped her head toward Scott. "Thanks for your part in saving his life."

"You're welcome. I'll let you both get some rest. See you tomorrow." He pulled her to him and gave her a tight hug because having a mask on didn't lend itself to kissing.

Hannah was returning to Jake's room after breakfast the next morning, and noticed the door stood ajar. Someone was talking to Jake. She recognized the rich voice. Jake giggled. Her pulse went into overdrive.

She gowned up and pushed the door open. Scott sat in the rocker with Jake in his lap. Scott had his mask pulled down to his chin, and Jake was busy feeding Scott cereal.

Hannah's heart stopped, and lurched again. It could be a Norman Rockwell picture. Jake let out a squeal of joy every time Scott lost a piece inside his mask. *Scott would make a wonderful father. If he would only believe that.*

He pulled at her heartstrings. Was he beginning to care for Jake less as a patient and more as a son? Would he ever consider being a parent of a heart patient when he worked with them all day? Dared she hope so?

Scott smiled up at her. "Hey. Jake woke up when I came in, and I didn't want to leave him here by himself."

"I went down to the cafeteria for breakfast. I thought he'd sleep until I got back."

"Would you like some of ours?" Scott asked.

She noticed Scott made no effort to hand Jake to her and Jake was content to stay where he was as well. Their coloring was close enough they could be family.

Jake offered the plastic bowl of cereal to her. Some fell to the floor. Both males laughed.

"Which ones are you guys giving me? The cereal off the floor or that in the bowl?"

Jake brought the bowl to his chest in a protective manner.

"The floor must be it," Scott said, with a grin. "Jake, I think we could be nicer to your mom."

Jake shook his head.

"I can see you're feeling much better this morning," Hannah told Jake. "Maybe too good. Dr. Mac might have done too fine a job on you." Hannah smiled at Scott.

Her heart swelled with the contentment of seeing her son so happy and comfortable with Scott. Hannah couldn't believe how quickly it had happened.

Jake and Scott had bonded. It would make it even harder when Scott stepped out of their lives. With all her heart she wanted this moment to last. But could it? Would Scott allow it? She didn't want Jake hurt by becoming too attached to Scott. That feeling she was very familiar with. Jake didn't need the loss of another man in his life.

"He's acting like a mischievous boy should," Scott said as he took another offered piece of cereal. Jake continued to stuff Scott's mouth with more than it could hold. He chewed and swallowed the mass before he rose with Jake in his arms. "Well, I've got to finish rounds."

Jake complained when he was handed over to her.

Reaching out, Scott tickled Jake's belly. He

squealed. "I'll be back to see you soon, bubby." Scott gave her a quick kiss on the lips.

Had she wanted to see a wistful look in Scott's eyes? Had it really been there?

Jake's day nurse entered soon after Scott left. She checked Jake's vitals and adjusted the settings on the monitors.

"Looks like Jake's doing great. He should be going home soon," the nurse said with stethoscope in hand as she prepared to listen to Jake's chest. "Dr. McIntyre's a great doctor. We're going to miss him when he leaves."

Bile rose in Hannah's throat. Her heart skipped a beat. She stopped rocking and sat up straight. "Leave? Where's he going?"

It was happening again. Scott was going to leave without saying anything to her again.

"The rumor is he's been offered a position as head of a transplant program in Dallas. He'd be starting the program from scratch, which is a big deal if you're a transplant surgeon," the nurse replied in an offhand manner.

Hannah's shoulders sank. Leaving? She couldn't believe Scott hadn't said anything to her. Why hadn't he?

She shouldn't have expected more, hoped for

more. He'd made no promises. Hadn't he made it clear where he stood the afternoon they'd spent in bed? She hadn't wanted to accept it.

"When's he supposed to leave?" Hannah made an effort to make the question sound nonchalant, despite the tightness in her chest.

The nurse adjusted the blanket over Jake. "Soon, I think. It's pretty much a done deal, I understand."

Hannah not only wanted Scott around because she loved him but because he was Jake's doctor. It gave her a sense of security to know Scott was close by if Jake needed him.

"Dr. Mac is such a great doctor I can't imagine him not getting the job." The nurse looked at her. "Uh, are you all right, Ms. Quinn?"

Hannah nodded, her stomach rolling like a ship in a storm.

"I thought you knew," the nurse said in an unsure voice.

"No, I didn't know and I'm concerned for Jake. Who'll care of him if Dr. McIntyre is no longer here?"

"Oh, don't worry there. We've other great doctors." She patted Hannah's hand, gave her a bright smile and went out the door.

A tear rolled down Hannah's cheek as she slowly started rocking again. It was the same old scene of the same old play. Scott hadn't changed. He planned to leave without saying a word. Again.

She knew what she had to do. End it.

Scott had managed to get out of the OR earlier than he thought possible and had every intention of spending the extra time with Hannah and Jake.

He took a few minutes to stop by his office to check his mail. While there he received a call from Dallas. Despite the short notice, they wanted him to fly out to speak with the committee the next day. Thankfully, his patients, including Jake, were doing well enough that he could agree. He made some quick travel arrangements.

He'd put off telling Hannah about Dallas because it wouldn't have mattered by the time he thought he would be moving. She would've gone on with her life, making it a non-issue.

Scott couldn't believe how fast Hannah had become important to him. Jake too. A chance to be with someone like Hannah didn't come along more than once in a lifetime. Well, maybe twice.

He knew what he was letting go of, but still he had to do it.

In another few days or so Jake might be going home. Scott's relationship with Hannah would change then anyway. With Jake recovering, she wouldn't need him any more.

Could he and Hannah maintain a long-distance relationship? Would seeing her occasionally fill his need for her? He didn't think so. It didn't matter he had to be a different person than he was for it to ever work.

Hannah didn't stand to greet him when he entered and closed the door to Jake's room behind him. She continued to hold Jake and rock.

Scott leaned down to kiss her, but she only offered her cheek. "How's Jake been doing today?"

"He's had a great day." She sounded pleased, but the words were stiff. She didn't look at him.

Was something bothering her? Jake's nurse had said nothing about there being a problem when he'd stopped at the nurses' station. "Hannah, is something wrong?"

Hannah looked up at him. "Why didn't you tell me you were planning to move to Dallas? Was it a secret? You didn't have to hide it from me. You've made it perfectly clear we have no ties on each other. I understood. But *friends* don't keep secrets."

The knot forming in his chest ached. There were ties between them, but he couldn't tell her that. Scott raised his brows. "How'd you come by that bit of info?"

"The hospital grapevine works for everyone." Her eye remained fixed on him. "So, are you leaving?"

"I've been interviewed by a hospital in Dallas. They want to start a transplant program. It's been my dream to head my own."

"When're you leaving?"

"I'm still in the discussion stage. But…I have to fly out first thing in the morning to meet with the committee."

"What about Jake?" Anxiousness crept into her voice.

His desire to help patients was already coming between them as he'd known it would. He didn't want her to live her life worried he wouldn't be there when she needed him. He was making the right decision, for both of them as well as Jake. "He's doing well. He'll soon be followed by Cardiology. My job is almost done." Scott tried to make the words sound matter-of-fact.

"I think, under the circumstances, it would be better for Jake if things remain professional between us. Jake doesn't need to get attached to you." She looked out the window as she spoke.

"Better for Jake?" His words came out softly.

She looked at him. "Okay, better for me. You're leaving, so what're we doing anyway? Having great sex? I want more, you don't or won't let yourself have more, so I think now is a good time to call it quits, before either one of us gets hurt."

Scott's chest felt like a band was being tightened around it. There was no longer an ache but a cavernous hurt. He had no one to blame but himself. "I told you—"

She shook her head, silencing him. "I know what you told me. The problem is you have issues that you need to resolve with yourself and your parents. I care for you more than you care for me. But I've been left behind or set aside for the last time. I have to think of Jake. He doesn't need to get attached to someone who won't be there for the long haul or want to see him make the first step. Jake deserves someone who will stick with him and fight for him, and I do too." The last few words had a bite to them.

Scott said nothing. He couldn't refute anything she'd said. He wished with all his heart he could.

"Stupid me," she murmured. "I'd hoped this time you'd feel differently." She gasped, swiping her hand across her cheek. "It's been fun while it lasted. Nice seeing you again."

Scott stood looking down at her for a long moment. He wanted to argue with her, but how could he? She was right. "One of the other surgeons will see about Jake while I'm gone. I'm sure he'll be discharged before I return. Goodbye, Hannah."

"Thanks for taking such good care of Jake and for helping me get through some stressful moments. I wish you the best in Dallas. Bye, Scott." The last few words had an iceberg chill of finality to them.

The pain of leaving Hannah was so searing and deep Scott found it difficult to breathe. For the first time in his life he was asking if he was doing the right thing.

CHAPTER TEN

HANNAH'S next few days were spent preparing to take Jake home. Hannah was grateful to be busy because it left less time to think about Scott. She pushed thoughts of him aside the best she could. At unexpected moments, like each time the door opened, Hannah's heart raced, thinking it might be Scott. It never was.

She missed him. Hurt with the want of him. As disappointed as she was that he didn't need her, it didn't make her love for him disappear, which only intensified the pain.

Jake had his first biopsy to determine if he was rejecting the new heart the morning after Scott left. Jake would continue to have biopsies regularly throughout his life. Hannah waited in Jake's room while the nurse took him to the cath lab for the procedure.

Wringing her hands until they were almost raw, Hannah watched the clock as an hour crawled by.

Dr. John Reynolds, the cardiologist now following Jake's progress, came in to see her. The test had shown no rejection and Dr. Reynolds planned to release Jake from the hospital the next day.

The news was like the sun coming out after a long, cold winter. Elated with Jake's recovery, Hannah's first thought was to share the good news with Scott. It was too late for that. The day turned gloomy again. Her sense of loss seemed as vast as the ocean.

Hannah was packed and ready to leave before Dr. Reynolds made rounds the next morning.

Once back at home, fretting over missing Scott took a backseat to caring for Jake. She gave medicine four times a day, checked Jake's blood pressure, temperature and weight at regular intervals. Feeding Jake took extra time, coaxing him to eat enough to gain weight. His incisions required attention as well.

Jake napped a number of times during the day, giving Hannah an opportunity to take care of her everyday matters. Bills arrived daily, and there were phone calls to make and return. Holding Jake became the highlight of her day. Reminded of how much she'd almost lost, she was grateful for each precious moment.

The nights were different. They dragged. Thoughts of Scott wandered in and camped. She relived all the wonderful times they'd had together, and yearned for his breath-stealing kisses, his body next to hers, his lovemaking. Despite being exhausted, it took hours for sleep to find her.

As the days lapsed into weeks the loss of Scott became a dull pain Hannah learned to live with. Like splinters, barely touched memories would flood back with a sting when she saw a tall man wearing a white lab coat or heard shoes tapping across a tile floor. Thoughts of Scott never completely left her.

No one liked being left behind, but it was a part of life. When had she become so scared of living? Chances had to be taken if happiness was ever to be found. She wouldn't have missed her time with Scott for anything. The pain was worth those amazing hours she'd spent in his arms.

Other people, sometimes more wonderful people, would enter to replace him. The secret was not to let fear close any door. She didn't want Jake to grow up with a mother fearful of life. She wanted to be a positive role model, strong, resilient, no matter what happened to her.

Hannah glanced at Jake as he swung in his swing and played with his bear. She wasn't the only one who'd been left behind, but her ex had given her a wonderful gift in Jake. Each positive report Jake received was a thrill. He'd grown since the transplant and was becoming more active. Still, the only time they left the condo was when Jake had an appointment at the hospital. She even had groceries delivered.

A thump of a toy falling on the floor and Jake's squeals made Hannah look up from balancing her checkbook. The toy Scott had given Jake had slipped from his hand. The little bear was Jake's constant companion.

Hannah smiled and leaned down to pick up the toy. Giving it to Jake, she kissed him on top of his head. "Time for meds, sweetie."

Hannah slipped into doing Jake's care as easily as putting on old shoes. Maybe Scott had been right. She should think about being a clinical nurse instead of working in a hospital. With a few extra courses, she could work with children. Perhaps working with transplant families would be a good place to consider. With leave pay still coming in for a while longer and her savings in fair shape, she had time to look into jobs when Jake had recovered enough to be left with a sitter.

Jake had been given a second chance at life and she planned to live her life to the fullest, for her sake as well as Jake's.

One afternoon the doorbell rang. Hannah answered it and found a delivery man there.

"Hannah Quinn?"

A huge box sat at her feet with the word "Fragile" written across the top.

"Yes, but I'm not expecting anything."

The man in the brown uniform smiled at her, and handed her an electronic device for her to sign. The return address indicated it was from one of the best gift shops in the area. There had to be some kind of mistake.

Hannah pulled the box indoors and cut through the packaging tape. Picking up one of the items in the container, she removed the plastic bubble wrap. Beneath it, she found a teacup from the set she'd admired at the fundraiser. Gently, she set it back with the rest of the set.

Reaching for the invoice under another item, she located a phone number. Calling the store, the manager explained she couldn't return the set because it had been donated to the hospital. Her name had been identified as the highest bidder.

Hanging up the phone, Hannah sat staring at the box. Scott must have bid on it when she'd gone to call about Jake.

She removed each piece with loving care until the completed set was arranged on the coffee table. Spying a white gift envelope pushed against the inside wall of the box, she pulled it out. Opening the card, she read: *"Don't even think about returning it. Enjoy. Scott."*

Hannah's hands shook and her eyes watered as she held the envelope to her chest.

Scott drummed his fingers on the desk as he waited to be connected with Dr. John Reynolds.

"Scott, how you doing?"

"I'm working more hours than should be humanly possible. What I was calling about—"

"You want to know how Jake Quinn is doing."

He was too transparent. John had to know Scott was checking on Hannah too. "Yeah."

"He's doing as expected, like I've told you every time you've called. His mom is taking excellent care of him."

"I appreciate the report." Scott smiled. Jake

was doing great. Was Hannah? He couldn't ask. But if Jake was getting better, Hannah had to be happy. He'd have to find contentment in that knowledge.

"I'll be in Atlanta in a few days to clear up some business. I'll stop by."

"Sounds great. I'd like to hear firsthand how your program is shaping up," John replied, and Scott rang off.

Maybe he should make arrangements to see Jake while in Atlanta. After all, Jake had been his patient. Who was he kidding? He wanted to see Hannah. Needed to see her.

Scott shouldn't have had time to think of Hannah with the amount of work he'd done in the last two months but she crept into his thoughts continuously. During meals, he thought of their shared ones. At night, it took him hours before sleep found him. Even after he fell asleep, Hannah filled his dreams. He ached to touch her and ached to have her touch him.

His hunger for her hadn't died. If anything, it had intensified.

For the first time in his life he wanted more than to be a great heart surgeon. He wanted Hannah. And Jake. Wanted to be a husband, father, a family man. He would do whatever was necessary to convince Hannah to take a chance on him. Without Hannah and Jake, nothing mattered.

Hannah had gotten his attention about more than setting his priorities in regard to work. He needed to set things right between him and his mother. Hannah would expect that, want that for him.

With Hannah as his life partner he could find that balance between his professional and private life. She had already helped to do that. Hannah would keep him centered, support him, while at the same time reminding him of what was really important. They could make it work—together.

He wanted it all. Would fight for it, beg for it if he had to.

But would Hannah have him?

"We need to hurry honey or we'll be late," Hannah said when she hiked Jake further up on her hip as they went down the hall of the hospital. Jake, with a mask covering his mouth, looked like a miniature doctor as he bounced along in her arms.

"If Dr. Reynolds says you can go out in public, we'll stop and get some ice cream on the way home," she promised.

Absorbed in her conversation, Hannah didn't notice the man standing next to the door of the pre/post cath lab. She reached for the doorknob.

"Hannah."

Her breath caught. Had her name ever sounded sweeter? Her thoughts swirled, and her blood hummed. She looked up into the most beautiful blue eyes she'd ever seen.

"Hello," Scott said.

"Hi."

"Dr. Mac," Jake squealed and reached out to him.

"Hi, big guy." Scott opened his arms to take Jake. He jerked toward Scott in his eagerness to be held by him. Hannah let Jake go to him. "You look like you're doing well."

Hannah gave up trying to slow her heartbeat. "What're you doing here?"

"I'm visiting. I had a few loose ends to take care of in Atlanta."

"Oh." Hannah tingled from the tip of her fingers to the ends of her toes. Now was the time to sound intelligent. *Talk to him.* "By the way, congratulations. I heard you got the job you were after. That's great." She meant it. She was proud of him. He was an outstanding surgeon.

"Thank you." Scott studied her a moment. "It's good to see you." He captured her gaze. "You look wonderful."

Her heart fluttered, his words a soft caress.

Scott stepped forward, tentatively reaching out a hand to touch her but not doing so. Jake demanded his attention by pulling on Scott's tie.

Sharp disappointment filled her at the abandoned connection.

Jake put out his hand, showing Scott his toy.

"What've you got there?" Scott asked. "Is that Bear?"

Jake looked at the toy and smiled, pulling it closer to his side.

Hannah had tried for weeks to replace the little toy with another one, but Jake had refused. He had to have Bear with him when he came to the hospital or when he fell asleep. For Hannah, the toy had been another constant reminder of Scott.

"Does Bear go everywhere with you?" Scott asked.

Jake thrust the toy at Scott. He studied it. Looking up at Hannah, with a twinkle in his eye he said, "Bear has gotten a lot of wear."

"Jake won't let him out of his sight." She didn't meet Scott's gaze. Instead, she focused on his broad smile as he returned the animal to Jake.

"Um...I'm glad we ran into you," she said. "It's nice to—"

"You didn't run into me. I've been waiting on you."

A stream of warmth Hannah hadn't felt in months raced through her. She didn't trust herself to say anything, so she just waited.

"Could we meet somewhere and talk?"

"I guess so." She brushed Jake's curls back as he squirmed in her arms. "How long are you going to be in town?"

"Until tomorrow."

"Would you...uh..." she'd promised herself she'd take chances "...like to come to dinner tonight? I owe you one or two." If he said no, could her heart stand it?

A look of surprise crossed his face before the grin she loved so much found his lips. "I have some meetings this afternoon but I'll make it work. Thanks."

Delight filled her at the sparkle of pleasure in his incredible eyes. "Six okay?"

"I'll be there."

She returned his smile with a bright one of her own. Hannah reached out to take Jake again. "We have to go. They're expecting Jake for a biopsy."

When Jake whined about having to leave Scott he said, "I'll see you this evening buddy. We'll play then."

Her hand shook as she opened the door of the cath lab.

Hannah shifted the candle a little to the left, then moved a book back to its original spot on the end table. She'd blurted out her invitation to Scott without thinking it through. The delivery boy had had to make two trips from the grocery store before she'd had everything she needed for the meal. The boy's face had brightened at the large tip he'd received on the last trip.

After trying on a couple of outfits, Hannah settled on a pair of jeans and a peach-colored sweater. The one she'd been told looked particularly nice on her. Tonight she wanted to appear at her best.

Hannah wouldn't let her hopes get out of hand enough to expect things to be different between her and Scott. She wanted to pull off the evening without seeming pathetic or needy. If he wanted some kind of relationship more than friendship but less than marriage, would she take it?

With a final check in the mirror, she went to the kitchen to finish preparing their meal. She was preparing to put the shrimp with white sauce on the linguine when the doorbell rang. With a deliberate movement she laid the spoon down. She adjusted her sweater at her waist and walked to the door. The bell rang again. Jake squealed as she passed, and she stopped to pick him up. With more flourish than intended, she opened the door.

Scott stood on the front stoop, shifting his weight from one foot to the other as if he thought she might not let him in. He didn't look like a self-assured surgeon. Instead, he appeared uncomfortable. Surely he wasn't uneasy about seeing her again.

Had anyone ever looked more appealing? Dressed in a green knit shirt and tan slacks he filled out perfectly, Scott had never looked better, which was helped by the fact she'd missed him so desperately.

Her stomach quivered. Scott was there.

His smile reached his eyes before his gaze fell away. He ran his hand through his hair in that uneasy gesture she recognized. What could he possibly be nervous about?

Shifting Jake to the other hip and stepping back, she said, "Please come in."

As Scott entered, he cleared his throat and said in a raspy voice, "For you." He handed her a small gift bag.

He reached for Jake. "Why don't you let me take Jake while you finish supper?"

Hannah wasn't surprised when Jake gave no argument to switching rides. Jake had bonded with Scott. She left the room to the sound of her son's laughter as Scott sat Jake on his foot to play This Little Horsy. A feeling of rightness washed over her.

In the kitchen, she poured the noodle mixture into a bowl. She turned to the bag Scott had brought her and pulled the light blue tissue paper out. Inside she found a tin of tea leaves and a tea diffuser in the shape of a house. Warmth filled her. The gifts were perfect.

At the sound of footsteps behind her, she turned.

Scott, with Jake in his arms, stood in the doorway. Scott appeared less out of sorts as he stood there than he had at the front door. It was as if

Jake had soothed his anxiousness. Scott looked like he belonged in her home. "I thought you could use them with your teaset."

"I love them." She beamed, hoping her smile showed all the delight she felt. "I should've said thank you for the teaset earlier. It's beautiful. You shouldn't have done this either." She dangled the diffuser from two fingers. "Did you pick it out yourself?"

He smiled. "No. The lady at the store helped me. I thought you'd appreciate them more than a bottle of wine."

"I do. They're wonderful."

Scott tickled Jake's belly, causing him to giggle. Looking down at him, he said, "Amazing, aren't they? How tough and resilient children are."

"Yes. Jake, come on. It's time to eat." She reached to take him but he clung to Scott.

Scott grinned. "Where does Jake sit?"

Hannah pointed to the highchair next to the table.

Their meal was pleasant, because she and Scott both focused their attention on Jake. Hannah enjoyed having a man at her table but she had the feeling Scott was anxious about something. Was she reading too much into him being there? He'd said he wanted to talk. The anticipation kept her on edge and apparently he was too. The one time she relaxed and he did also was when she asked Scott about his new job and got caught up in his excitement.

"I've been working a lot of hours and hiring staff. I've also had to spend time writing procedures and going to meetings, which aren't my favorite things. But I think we'll have a great program that will help many children."

"You must be very busy." Probably far too busy to have thought of her.

"Yeah. It's been nice to get away for a few days."

The meal completed, Scott helped her clear away the dishes and clean the kitchen while Jake played with a pot and spoon. Scott watched TV while Hannah got Jake ready for bed.

As she rocked Jake to sleep, Hannah sensed Scott's presence. She glanced at the door and found Scott leaning against the frame with his arms across his chest. He had a solemn, contemplative look on his face. What was he thinking?

Happiness had filled her at having Scott there, but by the way he was acting it had been only to see how Jake was doing. Was he here to say goodbye for ever?

Hannah continued to move back and forth despite being hyper-conscious about Scott's presence. Jake shifted in her arms as if he was responding to her reaction to Scott. When Jake eyelids lowered, she kissed his sweet-smelling forehead and started to rise. Scott stepped over and took Jake, gently laid him in his bed.

Hannah joined Scott at Jake's bedside. "Thank you for this. For these precious moments I might not have had."

Scott offered his hand, and she placed hers in his. He smiled as he laced his fingers through hers and gave them a gentle squeeze. "Hannah, can we talk now?" His words were soft and earnest. Without releasing her hand, he led her to the living room. At the sofa, Scott said, "Let's sit."

To Hannah's disappointment, he took a chair opposite her. Balling her trembling hands in her lap, she mustered up her courage. Hadn't everything already been said between them? He'd given no indication he'd change his mind. Supper had been two friends sharing a meal.

"I was surprised to see you at the hospital today. I'm so glad your new job is going well. I know they're glad to have you. Jake's growing and happy. I'm so proud of him."

Scott chuckled and moved over beside her. "Are you almost done? Can I speak?"

He smiled at the glow his comment brought to her cheeks. His heart lurched. *She hasn't shut me out entirely.* Was she as unsure as him? Maybe he had a chance.

"I was just trying to see how—"

Apparently she wasn't going to be quiet until he did something to get her attention. His mouth came down to claim hers, tugging at her full bottom lip until she opened for him. Scott registered her hesitation then acceptance and the moment she returned his kiss with complete abandon. He'd come home. With Hannah was where he belonged. What they shared weeks earlier still smoldered between them, and found oxygen again.

Before the kiss went beyond his control, he had to talk to her. Know what she was feeling. If she would take a chance on him—again. Scott ran his hands up Hannah's arms, cupped her shoulders, and put her away from him. Their lips remained inches apart. She made a small sound of protest, which added fuel to his already raging desire.

"I want…" Her eyes shined with a longing begging to be filled.

He smiled. "What do you want, honey?"

"You." The word came out like a caress.

Scott watched with pleasure as her face went crimson. "I want you too, but we need to talk first." He gave her another quick kiss, resisting the urge to take it deeper, despite Hannah's efforts to draw him closer.

Looking as if she'd been in a dream and reality had returned, she scrambled away and put some space between them. Her eyes were wide, her cheeks flushed and lips full. She'd never looked more beautiful, more desirable. His body throbbed for her. Battling the hunger roaring in him, Scott had to let her go. He couldn't carry on a rational conversation with her sitting so close to him.

He took one of her hands in his. Absently, he moved the pad of his thumb over the back of her hand. "We need to talk."

Her green eyes searched his, weary. She looked unsure. He'd not meant to make her feel anxious.

"I've been a plan follower all my life. The plan was working well until you showed up again. My life was no longer as clear cut as it had once been. But you didn't demand anything. You were strong and supportive of me even when your own child was sick. You understand the work I do and why it drives me. It has been made clear on more than one occasion you're nothing like my mother.

"Even when I woke you in the middle of the night, coming home late, you welcomed me, comforted me. I hadn't known how much I'd missed that in my life until then. I've realized that I share many wonderful traits with my father but I don't have to be like him in all ways. He should have set priorities, learned to say no, taken on a partner when he saw that his marriage and family were suffering.

"When I went to Dallas I knew I'd miss you but I had no idea how much. I ached with it. I dream about how nice it would be to come home to you and Jake every night. The comfort you would offer after a long, tough day." He grinned. "Or days. You wouldn't make unreasonable demands I couldn't meet. You would just take me in your arms and hold me."

Her eyes glistened with tears, and she squeezed his hand.

"I thought getting the position in Dallas would make my life perfect. It's everything I've worked for, sacrificed for. Today and this evening when Jake came so trustingly to me I knew I wanted to be his father, to feel that love every day. I couldn't return to Dallas without telling you how I feel. No job is worth sacrificing you for. Without you and Jake it means nothing. The most important thing in life has been missing in mine, and I found it with you and Jake. I want to settle down. Have a wife and a family.

"I want you and Jake. For Jake to have brothers and sisters. I wanted *that* with you. I love you."

Her lips parted and her eyes remained fixed on his. A knot of fear formed in his chest. Why didn't she say something? Had he misread her kisses?

With a sudden tiny squeak Hannah threw herself at him, wrapping her arms around his neck. Scott pulled her tight, his lips meeting hers in a searing kiss.

Her mouth left his, to slide across his cheek to his ear. "I love you so much. It almost killed me when you left. Please don't ever do it again."

His lips found hers again, the contact a gentle stroke of promise. He broke the kiss and looked straight into her eyes. "I know you have good reasons for being afraid I'll leave, but if you'll take a chance on me, I promise never to leave you again." His tone held all the sincerity he felt.

The kiss that sealed the pledge was sweet and spicy. After long, perfect moments Scott released her and his hand came up to brush her cheek.

Hannah's lips touched his palm.

Closing his eyes and breathing deeply, Scott labored to control his passion. Hannah was too close for him to think straight. He shifted, putting her at arm's length, but kept his hands on her shoulders.

With his gaze fixed on hers, Scott said, "I know I won't be around a lot at first and I'm already looking to bring another surgeon on to help. With you, I know I can find that balance between work and family. Together we can do anything. Please give us a chance. Marry me and move to Dallas?"

She wrapped her arms around his neck. "Yes, yes, yes." Scott's heart beat faster. A thrill better even than the one he had each time he saved a child's life.

He drew Hannah against him. His lips found the softness of hers. Her fingers fanned through his hair as she tugged him closer. Hannah opened her mouth, offering him the honeyed taste within.

With a murmur of satisfaction his tongue reached out and found hers.

When Hannah broke away Scott tried to pull her back, but she stayed him with hands to his chest. His fingers settled with a light touch at her hips.

She beamed up at him. "What took you so long, you big lug?"

Scott grinned. The feisty Hannah he loved so much had shown up. Tightening his grip, he brought her hips against his. "I fought it at first. But I knew I was a goner when I found myself calling the hospital a couple of times a week to check on Jake. I convince myself that I was only calling to check on Jake. When I realized that I wanted to ask more questions about you than him, I knew I was in trouble.

"Thanks to you, I've spoken to my mother and really cleared the air between us. She's even planning to visit soon. Things are better now between us than they have been in years. Surprisingly, she and Dad are even talking."

"I'm so glad." She leaned over and gave him a quick kiss.

His hands moved upwards until he could skim

the undersides of her breasts. His reward was a smoky come-hither look.

"I've been doing some thinking too," she said. "I believe you're right. I should consider working in a clinic situation. My appreciation for your skills has me thinking about how I can use my own."

"You know, I happen to need a good clinical nurse to work in the Dallas transplant program. Do you know anyone who might be interested?"

"I just might." With a grin on her face, she said, "I'd certainly have insight where others wouldn't." Her hands moved up over his biceps and across his shoulders. "Would *you* be my boss?" Her voice took on a Marilyn Monroe quality.

The combination of husky voice and twinkling eyes was intoxicating. Flirty Hannah sent a fire through Scott. He growled low in his chest. "You can count on it." He punctuated each word with small kisses.

Hannah guided his mouth down to hers.

Scott loved the way she couldn't seem to get enough of kissing him. As her lips traveled along his jaw, he said, "I've been living at the hospital the last few months. I've put off looking for a place to live in Dallas. Do you think you could help me find the right house? Maybe one with a big yard? A place for our kids to play?"

"I believe I can."

"In that case, I've something else I need your help with." At her expectant look, Scott chuckled. "But we'll need to find a bed."

"I know just where to find one." Hannah stood. Taking his hand, she tugged him down the hallway.

A feeling of pure satisfaction filled Scott. *I'm home.*

* * * * *

Mills & Boon® Large Print Medical

August

SYDNEY HARBOUR HOSPITAL: LILY'S SCANDAL	Marion Lennox
SYDNEY HARBOUR HOSPITAL: ZOE'S BABY	Alison Roberts
GINA'S LITTLE SECRET	Jennifer Taylor
TAMING THE LONE DOC'S HEART	Lucy Clark
THE RUNAWAY NURSE	Dianne Drake
THE BABY WHO SAVED DR CYNICAL	Connie Cox

September

FALLING FOR THE SHEIKH SHE SHOULDN'T	Fiona McArthur
DR CINDERELLA'S MIDNIGHT FLING	Kate Hardy
BROUGHT TOGETHER BY BABY	Margaret McDonagh
ONE MONTH TO BECOME A MUM	Louisa George
SYDNEY HARBOUR HOSPITAL: LUCA'S BAD GIRL	Amy Andrews
THE FIREBRAND WHO UNLOCKED HIS HEART	Anne Fraser

October

GEORGIE'S BIG GREEK WEDDING?	Emily Forbes
THE NURSE'S NOT-SO-SECRET SCANDAL	Wendy S. Marcus
DR RIGHT ALL ALONG	Joanna Neil
SUMMER WITH A FRENCH SURGEON	Margaret Barker
SYDNEY HARBOUR HOSPITAL: TOM'S REDEMPTION	Fiona Lowe
DOCTOR ON HER DOORSTEP	Annie Claydon

Mills & Boon® Large Print Medical

November

SYDNEY HARBOUR HOSPITAL: LEXI'S SECRET	Melanie Milburne
WEST WING TO MATERNITY WING!	Scarlet Wilson
DIAMOND RING FOR THE ICE QUEEN	Lucy Clark
NO.1 DAD IN TEXAS	Dianne Drake
THE DANGERS OF DATING YOUR BOSS	Sue MacKay
THE DOCTOR, HIS DAUGHTER AND ME	Leonie Knight

December

SYDNEY HARBOUR HOSPITAL: BELLA'S WISHLIST	Emily Forbes
DOCTOR'S MILE-HIGH FLING	Tina Beckett
HERS FOR ONE NIGHT ONLY?	Carol Marinelli
UNLOCKING THE SURGEON'S HEART	Jessica Matthews
MARRIAGE MIRACLE IN SWALLOWBROOK	Abigail Gordon
CELEBRITY IN BRAXTON FALLS	Judy Campbell

January

SYDNEY HARBOUR HOSPITAL: MARCO'S TEMPTATION	Fiona McArthur
WAKING UP WITH HIS RUNAWAY BRIDE	Louisa George
THE LEGENDARY PLAYBOY SURGEON	Alison Roberts
FALLING FOR HER IMPOSSIBLE BOSS	Alison Roberts
LETTING GO WITH DR RODRIGUEZ	Fiona Lowe
DR TALL, DARK...AND DANGEROUS?	Lynne Marshall